TANGLES OF THE HEART

ANASTASIA ALEXANDER

ELEGANT ELEPHANT BOOKS

Tangles of the Heart

Published by Elegant Elephant

Copyright © 2021 by Anastasia Alexander

Cover and ebook design by Molly Phipps

ISBN: 978-1948410014

Printed in the United States of America

Year of first printing: 2018

❋ Created with Vellum

Dedicated to:

Bill, thanks for being one of my dads.

Rick, this is my love letter to you.

CHAPTER 1

The snow twinkled as it tumbled from the sky. Snap. Freeze shot with a shutter speed of 1/400 to capture the crystals of each individual snowflake. The sun blurred and burst above the snow-capped pine trees. Green poked out of the weight of white, providing contrast to draw the eyes to the branches. This suggested a hidden richness and perhaps the dynamic motions of nature.

"Darlene, come in. You're going to get sick," Mom called from the back porch of the cabin, her hands cupped over her lips to carry the sound.

I snapped my next photo, wishing my mom would respect the fact I was an adult maybe just once. The picture blurred. I deleted my third attempt. Distractions always threw me off.

"In a little bit."

The sky still had billions of snowflakes dancing down, and I hadn't even shot the reservoir in contrast to the fall of the flakes.

"Now!" Mom yelled back with the order implied in her tone. "Austin will be here soon."

I missed my boyfriend, Austin Chambers. I missed his quirky side smile. I missed the cocky way he squared his shoulders, confident in his physique, even though he was not the tallest or most buff guy around. I missed the way he always smelled like a clean forest after a rain shower. But, most of all, I missed how he made me feel safe. Like I knew what I'd be getting each and every day, and it would never change. He was stability and safety, and that was exactly what I needed after the upset vibrating from my parent's split.

I slipped my camera back into its bag. Ever since my dad left my mom, I tried to do whatever my mom wanted to make her life easier. She had been through enough. The divorce really hit her in the core. I hated to witness such a capable smart woman crumble—losing her job, making a desperate attempt at survival by traveling across the country to hide in a cabin in Island Park, Idaho. It unsettled me that the woman I always looked to for safety could fall apart so entirely.

If I were living a normal life, that might not be so bad, but I wasn't. I was living in Island Park. It was Idaho. Think potatoes, *Napoleon Dynamite*, and a host of lodgepole pines. It sat in the lower southeast side of the state. Not Coeur d'Alene, that's too far north, too upscale, and a completely different place.

Island Park had no skinheads like those who lurked up north, just gigantic elk, rolling hills, the distant Teton mountains, and a bazillion buckets of snow that fell out of the sky for at least nine months of the year. Depending on the mood of the weather, sometimes ten to eleven months. Those years were always fun. Yes, I was being sarcastic, but not really. I love the beauty this place holds. Unyielding splendor. The isolation comforted me in its own way, most of the time. Well, part of the time, anyways.

Despite the beauty of open land with unpolluted royal-blue skies and organic nature, this area lacked people, stores, and things to do that involve interacting with others. Unless you call contact with your mom and her husband interacting with people. Personally, for me, that didn't count, and it went to show how low on the totem pole I had sunk, but it was the price I was willing to pay to be here because the awe was worth it, and I didn't know what else I wanted to do. Sometimes, though, when I stared at those beautiful Teton mountains, I'd wonder what lay on the other side.

We lived in a cabin, just like Walden, tapping into the mysteries of life. At least my mom said that was what we were doing. Boring. So, not having Austin, my only friend, around was a bigger problem than normal. I wasn't being dramatic. I was cabin sick and wanted someone around my age to join me here in the wilderness.

At the moment, the only thing I did to get out of the cabin was go to other people's cabins and clean them for my job. I have never dreamed of being a maid for work, but the pay wasn't bad and I liked making places look better than when I arrived.

I hiked in from shooting my photos and shuffled into the dining room. Across the open floorplan to the kitchen, Mom flipped through cookbooks. I perched on the window ledge of a long string of bay windows overlooking the wilderness, peeking out at the tumbling Snake River and the stately Tetons. Appreciation filled me, for this was one of those rare days warm enough that the wet snow didn't blanket everything that hid underneath.

I flipped through the images I'd saved from today's shoot to see if any of them were good enough.

Good enough for what? I thought with a touch of self-pity. It wasn't like I could do anything with my photos. They were just for me.

I moved through the day's shots. So far, a frozen image of the snow falling from the sky. I loved catching a handful of snowflakes frozen in a moment of time. It would remain just as it was, forever. Perfection.

A feeling of electricity shot across my skin at the thought of being able to achieve perfection even for one brief moment of time.

"Darlene, is Austin still not here?" Mom strolled into the kitchen with a cookbook in hand.

Thick gray clouds piled up over the distant mountains, past the empty rolling lands where the buffalo often grazed. I needed to join the outside country with Austin ASAP. I had been cooped up in the cabin life far too long. "Should be within the hour."

Mom hurried to the cupboard, found the salt bottle always within reach, and tossed a pinch of salt over her shoulder to ward off the impending bad luck—a British superstition. "The overcast day isn't a good sign." She pulled out a vegetable tray from the fridge.

My stomach lurched. Mom's superstition had a way of being annoyingly accurate a lot of the time. I didn't even want a hint of something going wrong today. I've been obsessing about how nice it would be to have Austin back way too much. Everything, once he got here, was going to be wonderful.

"Calm down with the superstition, will you? It's not helping my stomach or my racing thoughts any."

I never understood why she was so obsessed with superstition, but since the divorce, she clung to it to give her life a sense of control.

How silly to be nervous about Austin returning. This was Austin. We were besties. It made no sense for my stomach to twist like a used boat rope. I kept looking out the window every thirty seconds to see if he was arriving.

"You're a good girlfriend." Mom took a bite of a carrot, making a loud, crunching sound. Her skin had gone almost translucent, and the heavy lines under her eyes were gone. She looked younger than she had in years. Marrying Jackson had worked for her.

"If I were a good girlfriend, I'd be more understanding of him always being there for his mom."

Last time he left to do whatever he needed to do, I had been cold with him, arms crossed and short. Maybe he'd be upset with me for acting like that. "I could've been more patient about him leaving and saving his mom. I might even found it nice that he cared for her. That's a good quality in a guy."

Mom let that settle as she placed the vegetable tray back in the fridge. "You have to be you. Sometimes it's okay to not be happy. You don't want to be a Stepford girlfriend."

I rolled my eyes. Mom was about to charge into her feminist lecture. "I'll figure it out. Please."

She bent over to grab a rag out of the drawer but stopped to peer up at me. "Bu-u-u—"

She choked back her words, gritting her teeth. Two seconds later, she slapped her hand over her lips to keep her lecture in. Her face colored as she struggled to swallow her words.

"Mom, I know it's hard for you to not tell me what to do."

She sighed. "It is. I've been a mom for so long. I'm not adjusting to you being an adult very well."

I looked back out the window. That made two of us. No Austin yet, but the weather had changed to a slight drizzle, completely transforming the view from a snow haven to a hint of spring with pops of green color appearing out from the trees. "And you were a professor for so long, used to people being forced to listen to what you have to say."

"That's not—"

"Yes, it is," I snapped, focusing my attention on my mother for emphasis.

We made a great pair. I had a mother locked in control while I stayed locked in indecision.

"Mom, really, you got to trust me. I'll figure it out." At least I really hoped I would. I bit lightly on my lower lip.

Mom grabbed the dishcloth out of the drawer and wet it in the sink. I watched her clean, wiping the counter with more zest than normal. She wanted me to talk, and would feel better if I said something. I had always told her everything. I really didn't want to stop now.

"It bugs me how she controls him."

"How's that?" She wrang out the rag.

"His mom snaps her fingers, and he's there willing to do

whatever she wants. Come to Cali. *Boom!* There. Come to Tucson. *Boom!* There. Give me your college money. *Boom!* Gone."

Mom formed large circles with her arm as she cleaned the counter again. Her zest increased dramatically. She kept pausing from her work, peeking over at me, and waiting with her eyebrows raised—a signal to go on with my concerns. She reached into a bowl, pulled out a carrot, and snapped down on it. The crisp, biting sound broke the silence. Her eyes widened as she stood there.

She clearly wanted me to talk. To tell her what was going on with me.

"Maggie has a strong personality," Mom said.

That was a major understatement. Maggie was Jackson's ex-wife. So, the mention of her always made things awkward for everyone in our cabin. It was weird how intermingled we all were.

"How can Austin come from that?" I sighed, thinking of Maggie Chambers with her heavy makeup and the long blonde hair she loved to flaunt. "Austin cares about the environment and animals. All Maggie talks about is herself."

Mom didn't say anything.

"That just shows that Austin is a really good guy. For him to always be there, no matter what."

In fact, it was one of the things I loved best about him. He was reliable and steady. Not as flashy as other guys. I always knew what I was getting with him. He'd always be there for me. I pulled my bent knees toward my body and glanced out the window as a fish jumped in the river, stretching for the gray sky.

Hugging my knees even tighter, I said, "But he's been gone a lot."

Mom set the washcloth in the sink and came to me. She put her warm hand on my back. "I know, dear. It has to be hard to be here when there's no one your age."

I leaned into her comforting arms. "It's less lonely with him here."

Mom shot me a quick glance. "So, what are his plans? Will he be leaving for college?"

I jerked up straight. "College? No. Absolutely not. We're going to the Yellowstone Institute, remember?"

"Mmm…" Her soothing tone usually calmed me but, right now, it did anything but.

Maybe because she'd spoken my secret fear: that Austin really wasn't committed to taking courses at the Yellowstone Institute.

Mom made a loud swallowing noise. "Well, that should be fun." Her lips drew tight.

"We're not doing the institute because it will be *fun.*" I informed her, a bit haughtily. Yes, I could still be snappy at times, but at least I knew it. "It's important. We'll be learning how to preserve the park, protect the animals, and conservation principles."

In a setting with amazing opportunities for photography. I didn't mention that part. I didn't mention photography much anymore at all. Everyone was worried about my future these days—including me—and photography was a hobby, not a future.

Mom looked up, gleaming a comforting mom smile. "Good, hon', I'm glad it matters so much to you. Maybe you'll pursue something in the environmental field?"

She was not soothing or calming me *at all,* even though she meant well. It was my turn to hold in words.

Light glinted off the window from the kitchen lights—I could take great pictures right now. I wanted so much to be out there rather than inside, having my mom pressing me to make a decision.

My hand curled around my camera, but I didn't get up.

"I don't know yet," I mumbled.

Mom went to the dishwasher and opened it. "You're not doing the Yellowstone Institute because Austin wants it, are you?"

"Mom!"

I snapped, although this *had* been a new thing for me since hanging out with Austin. I did care about the Earth. Everyone should. Our only home was worth preserving, but I wasn't sure about making a career out of it. Secretly, I thought the classes would help me figure it out.

"Well, I just thought I'd mention it." Her voice sounded muffled as she unloaded cups from the dishwasher, avoiding my eye and a direct confrontation. "I mean, you're sort of drifting these days."

I put my feet on the ground and stared at my mom. "I'm not drifting! I practically run the cabin cleaning business since my boss left town. I take care of all the clients, making sure their cabins are clean as needed. Sometimes, I even collect the money, which wasn't in my job description. I work every day and... clean cabins... and..."

My indignant protest drifted off. Cleaning cabins, even if I'd practically ran the business since my boss moved to Seattle, didn't really qualify as a mission in life.

But I did have photography and Austin, and my mom and Jackson.

Austin was late, photography couldn't be a mission, and I was absolutely, one hundred percent, drifting. Like the snowflakes outside. Like artists waiting for inspiration.

A knock sounded at the door. My hand uncurled from the camera as I leaped to my feet.

"He's here!" I cried, running for the door.

Austin had saved the day again. Always taking care of me.

A warm golden light slipped in through the back windows, highlighting and shadowing the walkway. My heart picked up speed as I dashed to the door and opened it. A very tired version of Austin stood there with deep black bags under his big brown eyes, lots of facial growth, and a baseball cap on top of his head. He wore a sky-blue T-shirt, complete with stains.

He looked like he'd been through the wringer and wasn't up to hearing my problems. A romantic dinner in Idaho Falls seemed doubtful tonight. I didn't think he'd even be up for a stroll around the reservoir. The tiredness of his eyes screamed for a mattress and a long night's sleep.

The poor guy was exhausted, but he was here. He was here. I charged into him and curled up into his strong, toned arms.

Laughing lightly, he leaned down for a kiss.

I pulled back. He managed a smack to the side of my lips.

"My mom," I whispered under my breath, warning him we were being watched. My stomach fluttered with nerves making me want to crawl out of my skin. I knew we were of legal age, but it was still weird to kiss in front of my mom. I kept feeling like I would get in trouble.

He kissed me again, this time, catching my lips head-on and sending a tingle down my spine. He laughed. "Got you."

I stepped back from him to avoid more kissing attempts in front of my mom's raised eyebrows. "You seem tired but happy."

Mom crossed her arms though she appeared very content watching our reunion from across the room.

Austin paused before responding to my comment. "Yeah, I am. I think 'happy' describes it perfectly."

It felt weird. I had been so unhappy, and he had been the exact opposite.

"Everything go alright with your mom?"

His smile wavered before he caught himself and quickly smiled brighter. "Great. I did everything I could. She's now JT's worry."

Now, maybe, Austin would have time for me.

He cleared his throat. "Want to go canoeing?"

My mouth fell open. "What? You never want to go."

He simply shrugged one shoulder. "Want to go?"

"It's snowing."

"Wet snow. Most of it already melted." He gestured out the window.

I looked out. The trees were mostly green. "How?"

"The snow turned into rain as I came up. Come on, it'll be beautiful, and you're always saying you want to go."

That part was true. I had begged all summer with absolutely no success. But instead of feeling excited, a tickle of tension ran up my spine.

"What changed?" My eyes narrowed as I watched him. He was acting odd. "Ever since our canoe accident, you haven't been up for it. Why now?"

Austin shifted his weight and pulled up his sleeve on his coat jacket to peer at his watch. "It'd be good for both of us to get back on the lake." He zipped up his coat. "It's getting late. Want to go?"

His expression was irritatingly unreadable—stone-faced. If I delayed much longer, he might change his mind. I wasn't going to question him any further, even though he clearly was up to something. "Okay, okay, let's go."

I gave him a doubletake. Austin wouldn't suddenly, out of the blue, overcome his fear of the water. But if I questioned him much more on it now, he might change his mind. I hurried over to my camera.

"Just us, K?"

I studied Austin's serious face with pursed lips, trying to figure out what he meant.

He eyed my camera. "It'll be ruined if it gets wet."

"But—"

"Let's just have it be us, K? Not taking pictures and all that fuss."

A throb shot up my spine. I ignored it as I looked up at him. He was talking about my camera like it was a third wheel, which I guess it could be. I did take a lot of pictures sometimes.

He had periodically complained that I'd shift into a photo-taking frenzy and completely zone him out. That could be true. At times I did slip into a hyper-focus. I'd forget everything. Time seemed to just disappear.

Sometimes I'd go in a shooting frenzy when we were in

the middle of a discussion. I couldn't help it. We'd be talking. I'd be paying attention to our conversation, then I'd see a potential for a great shot, outside the window, along the dirt road, in the car, or wherever. When I saw the shot, I'd forget everything but that shot—wondering how it'd turn out and if the light was right. What would be the best settings on my camera? Stuff like that.

Austin cleared his throat.

I looked back at the camera. I might come across a cool picture in the dusk, but Austin wanted tonight on the canoe to be just us.

I let go of my grasp on the camera, leaving it sitting on the floor, feeling like I was abandoning a part of me. I hurried to Austin's side to join him for a canoe ride down the Snake River in the moonlight.

CHAPTER 2

*A*n hour later, we both faced forward in a forest green canoe, paddles draped over our laps and a broad smile on my face. The crisp fall air snapped at our bodies.

I breathed deep, filling my lungs full of the fresh, healing air. "I love it out here."

That often caused a smile and a lecture from Austin about the uniqueness of this wilderness and how efforts needed to be made to preserve it, but that didn't happen. Instead, Austin leaned back in the sinking orange sunlight. Had tiredness caught up with him from all his traveling? Or maybe dealing with his mom had exhausted him.

Our canoe had picked up speed, gliding down the river. Paddles weren't needed. The quiet engulfed us in serenity broken only by occasional splashes from jumping trout. I looked back at Austin again, ready to share a smile, but his narrowed eyes suggested he was strained about something.

I let my eyes feast on the splendor of the closing day. The dusk was highlighted in orangey-red. Pine trees transformed into silhouettes lining the banks in darker shades of gray as water spread wide around us.

A question sat with me about what Austin could be up to as we floated by mostly empty cabins. The navy-blue trees stood erect, like guards along the shoreline in the fading light.

When Austin became quiet and hesitant like this, it was best to wait for when he was ready to talk. Past experience taught me that if I pressed him, he'd clam up even tighter. Once, he barely spoke for two days until I finally found out he'd been turned down for a college application he'd secretly sent.

We had argued. I had wanted him to talk with me before he took a step that would basically tear us apart. He hadn't seen it that way and spoke about it like an opportunity lost. But all I'd felt was a relief he hadn't gone and sad that he had wanted to go.

We passed several more cabins, most of them near the shore of the river, and a lot of them sizeable empty mansions hallowed out from lack of use. Finally, he spoke with a hoarse tone.

"Darlene, I have something to tell you."

My stomach did a funny clench. I forced a laugh. "You missed me?"

"Yes, that but—"

"But, you don't want to do the institute with me?" I blurted, then caught my breath.

I didn't know where that came from. My breath stopped just from the thought of him not attending the institute with me. It made no sense if he wouldn't do it. He was the one who talked me into signing up in the first place. It was *his* dream, not mine. I was perfectly willing to make his dream mine, though, seeing as I didn't have many of my own yet. It also sounded interesting and important.

"What?" He put his oar into the water and steered us on a straighter course down the river. "I never said that."

My fingers curled tighter around the oar. "Then, what exactly?"

He let out a big gust of air. "Dar, let me talk."

I bit back my next words and waited.

He paddled two more strokes in the river. "Don't get mad."

Don't get mad? Blinking into the dying sunset rays, I flicked my fingernails against each other. The water splashed against the canoe as I waited to hear him out.

"As you know..." he sounded hesitant, "my mom and JT, her millionaire boyfriend, are together."

"Yes," my tone came out as tense as I felt.

He cleared his throat. "JT has taken a liking to me."

"You told me that before." My throat tightened. Managing my paddle, I slowly swung my legs to the other side of my canoe bench, so I faced him.

He glanced at me. His eyes slid away. "Oh, right."

"So, why are you telling me this again?" My hands tightened on the oar handle.

In the fading light, he didn't look so good. He'd taken on a greyish hue and hunched over.

"What is it, Austin?"

"He offered me a job."

The gentle waves splashed against the boat, rocking us.

"What did you say?"

"A job. JT wants me to work for him."

"Why?"

Austin shrugged. "He sees potential in me."

This made no sense. Austin hardly worked now.

"For what?"

"Hey."

I closed my eyes. Austin thought I was being rude. I wasn't trying to be rude. I just couldn't make sense of this. My thoughts spun in circles. None of what he was saying made any sense.

He was Mr. Reliable, not Mr. Change-His-Plans. He never changed his direction. His plans only changed when his mother snatched hold of him.

"Sorry," I said. "That didn't come out right. I'm just confused. I didn't think JT was into the environment."

Austin pulled his oars into the boat to let us drift.

"He thinks I'm a natural for the cell tower business. He thinks I'll pick it right up."

My jaw dropped into a frown line. "Cell towers?"

He still didn't meet my eyes. "Yeah. He thinks I have what it takes to be good. He wants to groom me."

I stared in amazement and fear. Who was this sitting before me? Not the guy who used to talk about the dangers to the environment of eating with plastic utensils. About being careful of our carbon footprint. About pollution and radiation and… it couldn't be. My reliable, safe friend, who not only protected the environment but *me,* had just turned into someone I didn't recognize.

"But they're ruining the environment. You always said that. *We* always said that."

His form crunched lower, but he said nothing about our mission.

A flash of anger pushed through the confusion and fear. "We've talked about the evils of corporations and what they do to our world, and now you're saying you're considering working for one of them?"

He shifted the oar to lay flatter on the bottom of the canoe. "The towers aren't going to go away no matter what we do, and JT's company is thinking about making them environmentally friendly."

It fogged for a second in the cool, damp air. "*Thinking* about it," I mumbled. It was hard to see. Everything blurred. "I can't believe you're saying this." My chilled fingers wrapped even tighter around the oar, the only solid thing I could find. "All those passionate talks about being the animals' advocate... all the dreams of helping the Earth... With one job offer by your mom's... your mom's.... whatever he is to her, and you give up everything you believe?"

My voice cracked. I brushed my forearm against my eyes.

He rubbed his face. "Darlene, it's not like that."

My eyes narrowed at his hunched form. "What's it like?" He was betraying us, our dreams, nature. "Would the job be here in Island Park?"

I was being ridiculous, but anger nipped at the best of me. I blinked. My eyes had gotten too watery from the chill.

"No." He cleared his throat. "The job offer is in Tucson."

"Tucson?"

"Arizona."

"I know where Tucson is," I countered.

Austin's gaze flickered over the darkening landscape.

Finally, it landed on the wooden paddle to avoid eye contact.

I took a breath of the clean, crisp air. The coldness pricked at my tightening throat. It grew harder to breathe. I stared at him.

He still avoided my eyes, shoulders raised as though preparing for a verbal blow from me.

My heart rate picked up from anger, from him refusing to look at me and thinking he needed to guard himself against my reaction.

The dull orange had sunk behind the rising gray mist of the river, casting dark shadows on my boyfriend, who had just returned home to shatter my dreams, plans, and future. We hit a rough-water patch as we skirted some big rocks on the riverbed. Its turbulence matched my heart rate. He planned to leave me. One way or another, he was going. That was what he was telling me with all this. That was why we were on the river in a canoe, now in the dark.

No dinner in Idaho Falls.

No institute classes together.

No sunset walks.

He was ending it all now.

I blinked hard to keep the tears inside. The night was too cold for tears to be a good idea. I closed my eyes to give me strength.

"Are you thinking of taking it?" I asked.

I waited for him to say, "Of course not, I have more morals than that. What do you take me for? Or, "Never. I'm staying by your side."

"Yes."

He said it so simply. No struggle. No hesitation as he

put a needle in the balloon of my future, of our lives together here in God's country, taking care of each other, avoiding the stress of corporate city life. I felt lightheaded and struggled to see clearly. Everything was moving in dizzy waves.

"Darlene, talk to me."

There wasn't anything to say to that except. *Good luck on your adventures,* but I didn't say that. "What?" My voice vibrated much worse than intended. It sounded hurt and pissed.

"It's a good opportunity. It's one of those once-in-a-lifetime kinds of things. I don't know if I can pass it up."

He was tossing away "our" dreams for a job with his mom's boyfriend. What did he want me to say to that?

"K. Does Jackson know?" I asked to give me time.

"I haven't told him yet, but I am sure he'll be fine with it. Well, mostly. He might not like me living so close to my mom. He thinks she's a bad influence. He doesn't say that, but I can tell from the way he flinches whenever I mention her."

That was something I could agree with my stepdad about.

We fell quiet, and I watched the rough water slip into gentle waves again. I tried to catch my breath.

After a drawn-out silence, Austin added, "I have the potential to make serious money like I've always dreamed about."

He was changing into a completely different person in front of me.

"When have you ever cared about making money?"

He looked away. The only noise was water lapping against the canoe.

"When did you ever care about money?" I demanded again.

His gaze shot to mine. "Always, Darlene. I've always cared."

"You never acted like it or said—"

"What am I going to say?" he snapped, his voice hard. "'Gee, I never want to be so hard-up I raid my kid's college fund like my mom felt like she had to do.' How about, 'I never want to be as desperate as my mom throwing herself at a man on national TV because she didn't know how else to survive.'"

He stopped short, breathing heavily.

I stiffened, unable to move with the news he'd just dropped like a bomb. The canoe rocked, like dust settling, from the attack.

I had no idea of any of that. I had no idea he felt like that. He had never said anything about it.

Not even a hint.

I reached out and touched his hand. It was cold in the winter twilight. So was mine.

His gaze came up, dark in the greyness. "You gotta admit, Dar, having money is a lot easier than not having it."

I sniffed, not ready to admit anything. "But... our dreams. The environment..."

"I can still make a difference." He straightened eagerly, causing the canoe to sway. "This is actually a real chance to make a difference, not just walking around with signs at a protest."

I frowned. "Make a difference, how?"

After another moment of silence, he shrugged.

I waited for him to say more… explain. But no, he was content to answer my question with a shrug. That was it. I wanted to scream at him.

The scream sat in my lungs—full of anger, fire, and rage —buzzing to be let out. It wanted to zap him until he woke up. Force him to say something, anything, not just sit there not answering my very important question.

He seemed okay not doing anything.

I blinked back my annoyance. This was probably what my mom felt like with me not making a decision on what I was going to do with my life.

I closed my eyes. I needed to calm down.

Finally, not knowing what else to do, I threw up my hands. "If you were working on some project like they are in India, focusing on protecting wildlife and humans from the radiation, then maybe I could see you wanting to go to work for them, but to just sell out for the money—"

"It's not about the money!" His shout echoed across the darkening river.

This was a big fight. I guessed when we erupted, we went all out.

He lowered his voice and took a breath. My heart pounded in my chest as I struggled to calm down. I blinked hard, unable to control the tears that pressed into my eyes.

The canoe rocked in the silence stretching out between us. He met my eyes in the moonshine, reflecting off the clouds and water.

"It's not about the money." He spoke softly like it was hard for him to say what he wanted to say."

I pressed my lips together, determined to listen to him,

but that didn't stop the question from jumping out, "What's it about?"

"Security. A future."

A light wind puffed past us. I said nothing. I'd have to give that some thought.

"Honestly…" Austin rubbed fingers along his oar handle, clearly searching for the right words.

I looked up at him, waiting for him to give me another confession since he seemed full of them tonight. "Yes?"

"The Institute doesn't give me—us—that."

I let his words settle in my chest. There was some truth to that. I wasn't happy about it, but I couldn't help but see he had a point. I also noticed he had hidden all these feelings and fears for all the time I had known him.

I had poured my heart out to him. Filling him up with my anxiety and worry, not knowing he had a secret world inside boiling with his own worries, fears, anger and panic… and maybe even desperation.

That made both of us emotional messes. That wasn't good.

I looked off toward the horizon to settle the flutter of desperation beating around in my chest. This stirred a lot of crap inside. Our relationship—friendship—was feeling really unsafe.

My gaze moved to stare at the steel bottom of the canoe with water running in rivulets as the boat swayed—back and forth, back and forth. Moving, but going nowhere and having no direction.

Austin shifted toward me. "I like your idea about the project in India." He put his hand over mine. "It's a good one. I could see what I could do. You know, talk to JT."

I shook my head slightly, knowing that wasn't going anywhere. Austin was making an effort to patch us up, so I didn't say anything to that offer. I didn't remove my hand from his.

"And I think… I think this is my way out. It's a chance to start over, to get some traction. And a future."

My ears rang from his words. I wanted to shake him and yell, "Wake up! What are you thinking?" This was crazy. Reckless. Not a good idea. But I swallowed back my protest.

"K."

Austin exhaled loudly. "Dar, what are you thinking?"

Water lapped at the rocky shoreline, and a distant owl hooted. Heat crawled up my neck. "So, you're leaving me?" I had meant to just say, "leaving," but "me" slipped out.

Austin carefully crawled over the middle seat of the canoe to sit straight in front of me. He reached out his icy hand and touched my knee, sending a chill through me. "Will you come with me?"

The wind had settled to a gentle tickle on our bodies in the shadowy night. I tugged my coat tighter.

"What does that mean?" I finally asked.

He sat straighter.

I took an icy breath in and released it, my mind reeling like a roller coaster.

He wanted me to pick up and move, just like that. *Snap.* Decision made. Life completely changed. I picked up the oar. My fingers ran against the texture of the wood.

Things took time to figure out.

The wind picked up as my stomach surged. I felt dizzy and unbalanced, wanting my best friend back, who kept me grounded and safe. Predictable Austin was always there, wanting to go on an adventure through God's country, calling our souls back to nature and primal selves. But now, I wasn't sure I knew Austin at all. He wasn't predictable. I mean, cell phone towers?

I wiped at a loose tear in the corner of my eye. He was leaving.

He stopped applying pressure on the tips of my forefingers. "This is about my future. What do you think?"

"'Bout *your* future?"

"Ours."

I flinched at his correction. Something about it felt just wrong.

"I've never been good at making decisions." That was how I ended up staying in Island Park—I had never decided what to do next. Then Austin suggested we save the environment together, and that sounded like as good an idea as any.

Austin tugged on my knee. "Come to Tucson. I want us to stay together."

The guy was confusing me. We'd never talked about our future as a couple—ever. We talked about taking classes together, going on hikes, that kind of stuff, but he, we, never defined our relationship. It was mostly assumed. Well, at least, I had assumed we were together. I wanted that... I think.

We kissed, we hugged, but never gave a label to what we had. We didn't even talk about whether we were seeing other people, although I wasn't, and I knew Austin wasn't either. I hoped... I swallowed the large lump in my throat, hard. No. I really doubted he was. But I never asked, and he never asked me. We just assumed, or maybe we didn't care?

Then, tonight, out of nowhere, he wants to define "us" by asking me to leave everything… my family, the mountains, the snow, the Snake River, and white billowy clouds, for a place called Tucson.

He wanted "us" to go on an adventure in the southwest. A wave a heat burned inside of me. This was an awful lot. It was hard to think straight. "Are you asking me to move in with you?" My voice trembled.

"No."

He had been too quick to spring that no. I blinked back moisture in my eyes, feeling like he had smacked me in the face. He had asked me to come along, but it felt like an afterthought—sprinkles on the cupcake. He could take or leave me coming, no real plan where I'd go or what I do, but he definitely was going.

A blackbird flew over us, and a glance at the moonlit shore showed we were not far from where we planned to climb out of the river. The darkness made the river threatening. The temperature had dropped as a sharp cold sliced into me on a gust of wind. We needed to focus on going home, not on the seriously life-changing decisions Austin just dropped on me.

More tears puddled in my eyes and threatened to escape down my freezing cheeks. This was not the Austin I knew. Out of nowhere, he decides to leave Island Park. He was stability. He liked to do the same things over and over. He went on walks at the same time of the day, explored Yellowstone on the same day of the week. He never changed. He wasn't Mr. Impulsive.

Boom. He changed on one trip. I crossed my arms over my chest. He had gone to rescue his mom before. He didn't change those times. But this time, he had. I peered at his dark shadow. Today, I didn't know who I had climbed in the canoe with, and I didn't know who he would become if he left again.

Water splashed against the canoe, rocking us. Once he reached Tucson and took on this job, would he change more? I looked over at him in the blackness. The clouds covered the moon.

"Darlene, say something," Austin's voice begged.

A coldness filled me, starting with my heart and spreading outward through my body. He was leaving me, changing everything. I was going to be alone in the wilderness with my mommy and her new husband and my boyfriend's dad. Fun. If that didn't make me a complete loser, I don't know what did.

"Have fun in Tucson."

"You won't come?" Austin asked. Strain vibrated in his voice. "We could do this together."

I fingered the top of the paddle several times. He sounded almost scared like he didn't want to go without me. I didn't want to be without him. I had wanted to deepen our relationship at some point, but I didn't think it'd be like this.

I had thought there would be... more emotion or connection or... What was the word? Passion.

Instead, he single-mindedly had decided to go on an adventure to see what was beyond the mountains.

I did want to know what was out there, too, but...

"How would it work with us doing it together?" He

stroked my knee as if I was a cat, and his touch did calm me a bit. "Jackson and my mom cover my expenses for housing. To do what you suggest, I'd have to quit my job, lose my paycheck, plus add the responsibility of rent onto my shoulders. Are you suggesting I get an apartment of my own?"

He squirmed in his seat. "Remember, we both agreed to not live with someone before marriage."

We had each made our declarations one day after church. Both of us had parents who made poor marriage choices, and we wanted to do everything we could to avoid that mistake, if possible.

The preacher had quoted statistics about how failed relationships increase with cohabitation before the wedding. Personally, I wanted to get to know someone without too much physical chemistry clouding my judgment.

I reached out across the canoe to feel for his arm. I had a sudden panicky need to touch him. He moved closer to me and held onto my arms. He leaned even farther toward me, rocking the boat as he kissed me with cold lips.

"I love you."

Did he? This conversation didn't give me much evidence of that, and he never said it before.

"We can figure it out, Dar. I'll go to Tucson first, and get you a job there, too."

I stiffened. "What? Me work for them? I'd be betraying the environment, too."

"Stop saying I'm betraying things." He took a deep calming breath, clearly annoyed. "I don't want to be apart."

I stared at him through the darkness. "That's different than saying you want us to be together."

He grunted. "Stop that. Same thing."

It wasn't, but I wasn't going to fight him over it. There was already enough tension between us.

"So?" he asked.

He was getting pushy. I decided to lay it all out, get to the point, and stop the round-and-round circles we were talking in.

"You're taking this job one way or another, no matter what."

He sat back on his canoe seat but didn't disagree. That was what I needed to know. I was an afterthought. I wasn't sure I wanted to be an afterthought. I'd have to think about this, but he needed an answer to what I thought about him going. Might as well give it to him.

"I'm not one of those girls who hold their guy back."

It seemed his shoulders relaxed in the dark. If that was the case, he heard what he needed to hear. I stared at the black shadows with trees dotting the shoreline.

"We need to get to shore."

CHAPTER 3

I stumbled back to the cabin, my footing uneven. I was a bit light-headed and teary-eyed. The wind had picked up, and it howled through me. Tucson? It was hard to stir up excitement about going to the land of cactus and heat, even if it was with Austin. The place sounded so distant and removed from anything I knew.

The back door creaked as I opened it. I tiptoed into the entry, not wanting to face my mother, nor Jackson, right now. A rustling came from the side bathroom. I froze. The toilet flushed. I continued to hold my breath, but that only caused the tears in my eyes to spill down my face faster. Water ran into the sink, then slowly, that sound ended, too. The door opened, and out stepped Mom, looking right at me.

"Oh, I didn't hear you come in," she said.

I remained frozen, which was stupid since she always noticed. Mom had been looking out for me, comforting me, and helping me stay safe since I was born. She saw everything. And I loved her for it.

And maybe I was a little tired of it. Maybe my mom always looking out for me was part of why I wasn't figuring out what to do with my life. Or going anywhere. And she wasn't going to like what I was about to tell her —that I was thinking of moving to Tucson to follow a boy.

My spine straightened. It'd be an adventure to go. I needed to do something to jolt me out of my rut.

Mom took a step closer to the bathroom light spilling out into the hallway. "Something's wrong. What is it?"

My throat constricted as I choked out the words, "Austin's moving to Tucson."

Mom stared at me with her soft eyes. "Why?" she breathed.

"A job. A corporate one."

"What? Wow. That's crazy."

She reached for me and stroked my back as I burst into tears.

"Oh, baby. I'm so sorry. Let's go make you hot chocolate and sit in front of the fire."

Hot chocolate might be just the thing I needed to feel at least a little better. It'd undoubtedly warm me up, and I needed that.

I followed my mom down the hall, taking halted and jerky steps as I swabbed away my tears. While Mom headed to the kitchen area of the great room, I took the couch closest to the fire, which happened to be the farthest away from Jackson.

I dashed him a look, wondering if he would be okay with Austin's new plans. Would he stop Austin from going? They didn't talk much, and Austin always stayed at his friend's house down the road so, unless Austin had called him on the way in, it wasn't likely Jackson knew.

Jackson looked up from reading his book and nodded.

I nodded back, not sure what else to do. I took a seat, curled my feet underneath me, and watched the flashing blue fire. The pitch black outside encircled the cabin, and a faint yellow light spilled from the antique lamp, cascading a soft glow into the cozy room. I zeroed in my focus on Jackson as Mom put the hot chocolate in the microwave.

"Do you know?"

He slipped his bookmark into his book. "What?"

"About Austin's job offer." I sniffed.

Jackson nodded, and my stomach knotted into a ball. He did call to tell his dad. I looked across the room at Mom. "Do you know, too?"

She pushed buttons on the microwave.

"No, she doesn't," Jackson said. "I just found out."

Mom tiptoed across the room like she was afraid of interfering in whatever was going on between Jackson and me. I didn't look at her when she handed me my hot chocolate.

Instead, I kept my focus on Jackson. His son planned to move away, and he acted like it wasn't any more interesting than the score of an insignificant game.

"Thanks," I muttered to Mom, sitting the cup on the floor by my feet.

She slipped next to Jackson on the couch. Their shoulders touched, signaling how they were there for each other. I tore my gaze away from them to look out the window at the Snake River, but could only see the soup-like darkness of night, so I turned my head to stare into the fireplace.

"He wants me to come with him," I said softly. "He thinks he can get me a job there, too." I watched the flicker of orange and blue fire burning its way through a log.

"Was he asking you to live with him? Get married? What?" Mom spoke with extreme tension in her voice, hinting at the panic she was obviously trying to stifle.

"Relax, Mom. He didn't want any of that. He wants us to be in the same town and continue to date."

"Sounds risky," Jackson said.

Risky? My gaze snapped on the dark shadows where Jackson sat. "What's risky?"

Jackson kept his eyes on the dying fire.

"What's risky?" I asked again, my attention glued to the quiet man.

Jackson shifted in his seat. "The lack of commitment makes it risky. Being in a strange town with no family or friends makes it risky." He leaned forward. "Both of you are still young adults, too young for a serious relationship. Neither of you is old enough to know what's best for yourselves."

My eyes flashed to him. "That's ridiculous!"

I jumped to my feet. I wasn't too young to have a serious relationship with Austin. Jackson suggested our relationship wasn't serious like his and Mom's. That we didn't belong together or, if we did, we didn't have the skills to make it work. My breath came hard and strong as anger stirred in my throat. "I know what's best for me."

My throat tightened so tight that if I didn't leave soon, I

wouldn't be breathing. I hurried across the room with no idea of where to go or what to do.

"Darlene?" Mom called out.

I didn't answer. I didn't want her comfort or excuses. Frankly, I didn't want to talk about it.

"Darlene!"

It wasn't in my mom's nature to let this go. "I'm hungry," I snapped back. "I'm getting myself something to eat."

To prove my point, I headed straight for the refrigerator and tugged open the door to glimpse all the food. There was a ham from last night. I loved its salty taste and grabbed for it until I saw the roast beef. It might give me more strength than ham. I could make a sandwich and drown my sorrows.

I reached for it, but remembered I'd been tossing around the idea of becoming a vegetarian to help the planet. And here I was, in a moment of high emotion, forgetting my resolve. Maybe Austin wasn't the only one selling out. I closed the refrigerator.

Mom made it to the kitchen, watching me. "Do you—"

"No," I snapped. "I can get a snack for myself." I could, too. I strolled over to the cabinet, eyeing the mushroom soup, beef stew, tomato soup, and chicken with rice soup in a can. Full of MSG. I slammed the cupboard shut.

"Jackson didn't mean to sound so gruff."

A pebble-sized lump pressed into my chest. "It's fine. He's wrong." My fingers curled into fists. "I'll prove it." The lump thickened as I thought about it. "I know what's right for my life."

I looked back at the shut cupboard. I wasn't even

hungry anyways. It didn't matter that I couldn't figure out what to eat.

Mom held out her hand. "Just let me say a few more things. It might help." She waited for me to respond.

I needed to cut off the pending lecture. "You've told me a thousand times that you made a mistake."

"That's true."

"You're too worried I'm going to be you."

A frown edged onto her face. "I could see how you could think that." She stepped closer to me as though to hug me.

I took a step back. "I'm going to decide on my own."

She brushed a strand of her brown hair behind her shoulder. "Whatever you decide, I'll support you a hundred percent."

I eyed her. "I doubt that. You might not like it."

"True."

I flicked a look at her.

She peered at me in earnest. "It's your life, baby," she said. "You get to pick your own path. You get to pick what's best for you."

The pebble grew into a stone and pressed hard into my chest. "Yes, I guess I do."

THE NEXT MORNING, thirteen minutes before six, a tap rattled the back door. Because I had barely slept, and because the sun had already started to stream its golden rays into my small room, I knew who it was.

Austin.

Just like old times. For the past year, Austin had come over early in the morning, and tossed a couple of rocks at my window, waking me up to go watch the sunrise with him.

All those other times, I had leaped out of my bed. Now, I held back, frozen, unable to push past the ice brick of emotions layered up inside me. I lay in an icehouse of conflicting emotions.

Angry—how could he just dump that life-altering news on me in a canoe?

Betrayed—how could he suggest leaving me?

Scared—how could he suggest I come with him?

But if he left… what would I do?

I was so riled up last night, I didn't even notice I wasn't hurt or heartsick at the idea of him leaving, just angry and betrayed and scared.

Definitely scared.

I pulled the covers over my head, not able to shake the feeling that once I slipped out of this bed, everything would change.

Knock. Knock. Knock.

My fingers curled around the cotton bedsheet.

He hit the side door louder with more insistence, apparently not caring now if my mom and Jackson heard him.

"Darlene!" His voice sounded loud and piercing.

I didn't move. Frozen. He wanted to talk.

"I know you can hear me."

My chest tightened from the lack of oxygen. If I didn't talk to him now, he'd come to my work or show up for dinner later. My way was running and hiding. Like I was doing right now under the covers. Like my mother did with my dad when things went bad. I didn't want to be my mother.

Clamping my jaw, I flung the covers back. The cold air hit me, sending a shiver through me. This wasn't going to be easy.

"Dar, we need to talk!"

Grabbing the first pair of jeans I could find on the floor, I yelled, "Hold your horses." With a lower voice, I muttered, "I don't get what all the rush is about." My pants slipped quickly on. I buckled them, my emotions still steaming. "You pretty much summed everything up last night."

I glanced longingly back at the bed where my blankets and sheets lay in a huge, tumbled mess. Sometimes it was better to just stay under the covers. Talking was overrated. There was nothing to talk about. Austin was leaving and "trying" to see if he could secure me a job so I could come, too.

What else was there to say? Probably nothing. I'd get this conversation over quickly then make it work early. I had a lot of angst to release while cleaning today. Transforming a room from a mess to clean would be a great escape.

I yanked on my T-shirt and headed toward the back door with my hair tumbling out of a ponytail. My bare feet were cold on the chilled floor. I cracked open the back door, shifting my weight. It creaked in the morning stillness.

Austin shoved his hands deep into the pockets of his flannel jacket, his shoulders jacked up close to his ears. He stood a few feet away, looking attractive with his hair poking up and sporting his shy smile. "Want to take a walk?"

My heart lurched, forgetting about my anger and wishing everything would go instantly back to the way it was. Those walks had been our thing. Out in the early morning strolling with only the birds to keep us company. I rubbed my eyes to remove sleepiness and glowered at him.

"I just woke up."

"I won't be able to sleep or sit still until we work things out."

He yawned. His eyes were puffy, and he did look awful. Somehow it made things better that he was struggling with this, too.

I held back the snide remark I wanted to make and instead said, "We can't have that."

Relief washed over his face.

I was going to make this conversation as fast as possible. Five minutes tops. All I wanted this morning was to drink a cup of herbal tea while standing out on the back porch to listen to the animals scurrying awake before I sprinted to work. I didn't want to hear all the excuses he had stayed up last night thinking of. I was in absolutely no mood for that kind of smoothing over.

"I don't have much time," I added just in case he was mistaking my kindness.

His mouth fell slightly open and confusion spread across his face.

"Work." I clarified.

His shoulders slumped. "Hurry then."

Several minutes later, I was bundled up in moon boots

and a double-layered flannel coat, treading behind him. The nippy air snapped at us as the first morning rumblings of creatures stirred. Austin grabbed my mittened hand. I tried to resist, but he held me firm and pulled me up next to him. "Beautiful day."

We made our way up the precipice that peered down onto the Snake River. We didn't talk much but, once at the top, we looked out onto the river.

The sky was still gray, as the rays of the morning sun hadn't quite made it up over the hill. Just like I hadn't completely woken up. Thick gray fog hovered over the water, casting a mysterious feeling on the scene. It mirrored my gloom.

The greens were muted, and the river tumbled on in a hurry to make it somewhere. I felt like Austin was the river wanting to go. At the same time, I lingered behind him, being pulled into the current of the whitecaps dotted across the river.

The fish jumped, busily snacking and excited. Watching them settled me. It was always beautiful here, but that didn't change the fact I was mad at Austin. He still was in the doghouse as far as I was concerned.

He walked along the ridge for a few more minutes. I followed but had to ask, "Where are we going? I have to get back soon."

He stopped at the top of a knoll and turned to face me. "This is one of your favorite views, isn't it?"

His face was paler than normal. He was pulling all the stops this morning. I took a deep breath looking out across the living Snake River with its energetic roll through the valley below.

"I really want you to come with me." A puff of chilled air slipped from my lips. His words were like air bubbles, soon to disappear. "You're important to me, and I don't want us to be ap— I want us to be together."

I shifted my feet and listened to the twigs snapping under my boot soles, not knowing how to respond. Bubbles of discomfort fluttered in my chest. He had never said anything like this before. I kicked at the twigs. It wasn't the right time. It felt too planned, too manipulative. Too "what he thought he should say."

He shifted his weight, apparently not comfortable with words, either. We were acting out a scene, showing what our relationship should look like, and it wasn't coming off right. I shoved my hands deeper into my coat pockets. Maybe I was being too hard on Austin.

He had never before told me I was important to him. That was big. That might be why he had dots of sweat on his brow despite the temperature. Yet, the timing of him telling me I was important to him today was just far too calculated.

I brushed at my hair, pulling it off my face. "You want me to move without any commitment?"

His eyes grew wide. "I— I don't know what to say."

"Yes or no would work."

He shoved his hands deep into his coat pockets. "Darlene, we're too young to get married. I just can't do that yet. Maybe next year when I'm making enough."

I looked away from him. I wasn't up for marriage yet either, but the way he said it didn't settle right. He didn't have to say so emphatically he was opposed to the idea.

"What's that supposed to mean?"

He lowered his chin to his chest "Things like that take time. Let's not rush it."

My eyes widened. "Rush it? You're accusing me of rushing it when the only reason we're having this conversation is because of *you*. I was fine with the way things were."

His shoulders hunkered down. "Darlene, you know what I mean."

I felt my head shaking. "Actually, I don't. We had a plan. We were following it. You changed it, and now you're talking about a new job, new place, moving—who's rushing?"

A thick silence fell between us, broken only by two birds chirping at each other.

He pressed his lips together. "I don't want to fight."

I sighed. "I don't either."

Relief flashed over his face. We agreed on something.

"This is one of those rare opportunities. I'd regret it if I didn't try. This is a good job. It would help me make money. Get in a good spot."

I kicked at a rock on the dirt and watched it tumble away. "I get that. Do what you need to do."

"Really?"

The hope in his voice caused me to look up.

"Really."

He smiled at me, and my body relaxed.

He shifted his weight as though shaking off the tension between us. "I know it's asking a lot to want you to join me and, even if you did come, you couldn't come right away. I get that."

He did? The familiar pebble in my throat started to ease

the pressure. I sniffed. My relief must have encouraged him to continue to talk.

"We need to get out in the world more. See how things are outside of Idaho. Get experience under our belts before we commit to a path."

The pebble thickened again. "But what about us?"

He looked at me with an unreadable seriousness. "We both came from broken homes, Dar. I don't want to rush anything. Rent is cheap there. Really cheap. Some of the lowest rent in the country. I can find us inexpensive apartments right by each other."

I breathed out a rugged puff of air. "I'm not making that much. It might be cheap, but I don't have enough saved for a down payment on rent..." My voice wavered. I didn't want to leave, and I didn't want to stay. I didn't want to be alone with Jackson and Mom and the cabins, going nowhere. But there was no place I actually *did* want to go. I didn't want to have to choose. I wanted Austin to choose, but now that he had, I didn't like his choice.

I felt twisted inside.

The sun created a hairline fracture of pink color along the edge of the horizon. I wished I had my camera with me to capture that sight.

Austin shifted on his feet. "I'll pay for your down payment."

"What?" My gaze flashed to him. He wanted to pay my rent? A small bird flew in the far distant sky behind him. He often helped out his mom, and now he wanted to help me out to be with him. Maybe he really did want us together, or maybe it was a habit of his to over give.

"Sure." He shrugged. "You'd be moving for me. It's the least I could do. I'll put down the first and last."

"You don't have that kind of money."

He shrugged again. "JT is putting me up. I can do that for you if I save. Plus," he smiled, "I actually talked to him about hiring you last night. He's interested. You'd be a natural."

I blinked. "A natural? At what?" I snapped, my frustration getting the better of me.

"Well—"

I shoved my hands deeper into the pockets of my jacket, hoping to grasp patience there while I waited for him to arrive at the point. He wasn't the only one who hadn't slept well last night.

"After our conversation, I called him and told him about your concern about the environment."

"You what?"

"Told him about—?"

"I heard you. Why would you tell your boss that? Why would you even be talking to him about me? That's weird."

Austin reached out and put his hand on my shoulder. "He's going to be my stepdad, remember? I was talking to my mom, but then she put JT on the phone."

I ruffled at the idea of Austin talking to Maggie about me. Nothing was private, apparently.

Austin took his hand off my shoulder. "He thought you made a good point."

"About what?" I struggled to keep up with the conversation.

"About the environment. He's going to look into it. He

thought maybe you could be part of the team that recommends changes he can make to be more pro-environment."

That was actually cool.

"He has to look into a couple more things, but he wanted to know if you'd come out in a month and talk to him about being on the team that will oversee it. He said he'd pay fifteen an hour, and you can work yourself up to getting benefits."

My mouth fell open. Austin had to be kidding. A person didn't just get a job offer from having a conversation with their boyfriend. That didn't happen. But this was a good one, especially if it meant I was helping good Old Mother Earth out. I could see myself working for a company helping with the environment. A step up from cleaning cabins.

His smile wavered. "That would give me time to figure out my job and find the options for apartments."

With a sudden motion, his iron arms encircled me, pulling me tight against him. A button from his flannel shirt jabbed into my face. "Darlene," he whispered, "please come with me."

"Why?" I muttered into the furry collar of his coat.

I wrapped my arms tighter around him to hold onto some sense of who I was in the middle of all this.

"Because we're best friends. We were there through our parents' divorces and remarriages. We even managed to have fun together through it."

That was true. We were best friends. He was the person I spent time with and talked to.

"You make it sound like we're brother and sister."

"Not quite," Austin said. I could feel the trembling of his heart in my ears as a little warning bell rang inside me.

Was it really so great between us? I tipped my face up and looked into his eyes. "But still no commitment, huh?"

He sighed. "Darlene... I don't know what you want. I can't propose."

I extricated myself from his arms. "I understand. That's fair. But I can't move to another state, following you around, without knowing we have a future."

His arms dropped. "So, you're not coming?" he said in a low voice.

I had a choice before me. I saw it now. It was the job, but it was more than the job. If I let Austin be the one to make a choice for me and allowed him to dictate the terms of our ambiguous relationship, nothing would ever be different between us. I knew that with certainty as cold as the winds blowing down off the mountaintop.

Maybe *we* weren't what I thought *we* were. Austin wanted me to go with him to Tucson but not rush our relationship. Maybe my stepfather, Jackson, had been onto something about his son not knowing what was best for himself. The idea had made me mad last night since Jackson included me in the comment, but... Maybe Austin wasn't so clear on where he stood with me, us, our relationship. And maybe I'd be a fool to go with the flow anymore.

The sun leisurely rose into the sky, spreading a whitish glow along the horizon. The Snake River flowed happily toward the ocean. A few buffalo across the river swung their tails and took a few bites of the foliage.

Steam from our breaths shot out into the crisp air, and

then... *poof!* Gone. I loved this view, this country, being here. I had to get out into this wilderness, maybe after work, and take more pictures.

This was some of the prettiest land anywhere. I could enjoy this view every morning. And most days, I did. Now, though, Austin wouldn't be here to appreciate it with me.

"If you really want to do this, go do it. If things are still working out for you, I'll visit in a month if we have an understanding about our relationship."

He looked baffled. "What kind of *understanding?*"

My stomach cinched like a massive fist had just punched me. I cleared my throat. "I think it's best our relationship remains open."

"Open?"

"Yes, open. Let's just see how it goes and if the long-distance thing doesn't work out, you just let me know, okay?"

Austin's mouth gaped wide as he processed this. "Does this have to do with your dad cheating?"

I stiffened. "No. It has to do with we're not ready for a status decision, so let's not make one."

"Fine," he snapped and pulled slightly away.

"Fine." I crossed my arms over my chest. There, I had made a decision. Points for me.

Austin pulled me close again. "I'm not dating anyone else."

I rested my head on his pounding, muscled chest.

"I don't want any other girl, but if you want to date others, you're free to do so. For my part, I'm only dating you. That's the commitment I can give you, and I'm okay if, for right now, you don't give it back."

CHAPTER 4

A month later, after Austin's and my uncomfortable conversation overlooking the Snake River, I found myself driving through a recently fallen batch of snow to Idaho Falls to board a plane en route to Tucson by way of Salt Lake City.

I wiped the sweat from my palms onto my jeans as I drove. My first real adventure out into the real world on my own. I let out a puff of air. I could do this. I knew I could.

The first plane ride, first real job interview, my first real consideration of moving away from my mom. According to Austin, the town hosted more than six hundred thousand people and counted the outskirts. The numbers climbed to above a million.

My stomach tightened as I peeked at the GPS, trusting the green dot would take me to the spot it promised. I hoped. I have heard grumblings that sometimes the direction locator wasn't always accurate.

The light dusting of snow squeaked under my tires. A

plow must have charged through recently. The mounds of snow on either side of the road let me know there was only one direction to go—forward.

I had shrugged off my gloves, scarf, and coat one at a time as the car warmed. Maybe I'd leave all of that in the car since I wouldn't be needing it in Tucson. Austin had raved about the warmth that wrapped around him like a toasty blanket.

The windshield wiper swiped at another dusting of snow that had piled up on the windshield. At this moment, being in that kind of heat was hard to picture.

A wave of nerves slapped me. I grabbed my phone and re-read the texts as I drove.

Austin: *See you soon.*

Me: *At the airport.*

Austin: *Yep.*

Me: *Don't be late.*

SMILEY FACE. That meant, okay. He got it. He wouldn't forget about me and leave me at the airport. I hoped. My stomach tightened. I had wondered what was over on the other side of the mountain. Now, I was going to find out.

Austin and I had talked almost every day—he called me.

"I miss you," he'd say. "When are you coming to visit me?"

Or, "You'll love it here. It's so different than Idaho. They have cactus!" He rambled on about mountains covered with cacti and how he'd never seen anything like it.

"Is there waterskiing there?" I asked once, curious about this new town.

"Waterskiing?" he repeated like he didn't know what it was.

But he did. We loved to do that together.

"Don't think they have that. Not much water. It's a desert."

"Sounds lovely," I lied. No waterskiing? No water? Cactus? Tempting. Not.

"It has lots of wildlife, though. They call it a living desert."

iI sounded like I could take unique photographs. It would give me a chance to explore a completely different terrain.

"How's the job?" I finally forced myself to ask.

"Oh, I love it. I feel like I'm in the middle of it all."

While Austin was in the middle of it all, I was finding myself in the middle of a lot of empty cabins to clean. Plus, lots and lots of white snow piled up like a massive fluffy pancake.

"You'll be in it, too," he said on our last call.

He had successfully convinced JT to fly me down to Tucson to interview for the new business team. I guess I was heading right into the middle of it.

As I pulled into the Idaho Falls airport parking lot, my phone rang. "Hi, Mom. Not there yet, just arriving."

She was being seriously overprotective about this whole trip. If she had her way, I'd stay by her side in Island Park, hiding from the world.

"Don't let them pressure you just because Austin wants you to be there. You don't want to be stuck doing a job you don't want to do."

I laughed at my mom's comment. "You mean like cleaning other people's cabins?"

Mom sighed. "Yeah, like that."

I parked in the almost empty lot. Mom thought her biggest mistake was orchestrating her life around my father when I was growing up.

"Mom, I plan on making my own mistakes." I pulled the keys out of the ignition. They clinked together in celebration of the unique mistakes I'd make.

I dug into my bag and pulled out my camera. Time to seize the beauty of my parked car. I was going to immortalize the accomplishment of my first trip off on my own.

I snapped several pictures at side angles, capturing the car dirty, surrounded by dirty snow.

Mom sighed heavily over the phone. "Okay, then. Don't feel pressured to take the job just because they fly you out there."

A single bird flew far up in the sky, riding the currents.

I freeze-framed the flight.

I wasn't going to do something just to make others happy.

I hoped.

I wasn't going to move there unless it was the right thing to do. I snapped a picture of the small airport that would fly me from Idaho.

* * *

I STUMBLED THROUGH THE AIRPORT, poked, scanned, and verified, then climbed aboard a tiny commuter plane. It seemed like the plane had just lifted off when it was time for me to deplane straight into the Salt Lake City airport. The noise and size made my head spin. My breath came rapidly until I finally found the hidden terminal that zipped down to Tucson.

The plane had been delayed thirty minutes, the announcer said, due to a late arrival.

The terminal filled with angry or annoyed passengers. Some immediately whipped out their phones.

One man muttered, "They better make it up."

I, on the other hand, sat in the midst of the outcry and watched the ripple reactions. A lady sitting next to me asked, "Does that announcement affect you?"

I looked at her, surprised. "I guess it does."

She sighed. "Me, too. I'm a local from there, so it doesn't bother me too much. How about you?"

I thought about it. I wasn't bothered by it at all. "No, not really." Other than it will be later when I see Austin, and maybe need to delay my interview. Funny, I hadn't seen Austin in a month. Last time I hadn't seen him for a week, and I had been so anxious to reunite. This time not so much.

I stood to wiggle my legs and to take pictures. I wanted to capture the frustrations on the passenger's faces. The kids moving around, smiling and oblivious, like they were in an exercise video.

I captured an image of a beautiful little girl with amazing thick black curls. She poked out her butt and shook it. I captured a photo of her as she started her next shake, right before she burst into laughter, wholly unself-conscious, and full of joy.

Just as I was shooting, Austin texted: *Can't wait.*

Twenty minutes later, I texted back: *Boarding.*

I gathered in the line like all the other sheep and waited for my section to be called.

Austin texted. Another smiley face.

The other passengers' expressions looked as blank as I felt. I found my seat and settled in, watching the people entering the plane. I couldn't help but think about the old TV show, *Lost,* where plane passengers were stuck together for years on a strange island after a crash.

What would it be like to be stuck with these people? I was thinking about this when a most beautiful cowboy sauntered down the aisle. I found myself gasping. Tall, his brown hat, plopped at a crooked slant on his head, almost brushed the roof of the plane. He was the embodiment of cowboy sexiness, which caused my pulse to increase just by glancing at him. He wore broken-in jeans that enhanced his lean legs and a shirt that fit tight across his broad, muscular shoulders. He surveyed the back of the plane where I sat, his crystal blue eyes seizing my attention. He had confidence and a friendly, natural air.

Certainly drool-worthy, he looked like one of the male models from the calendar magazines my friends from high school liked to hang up in their bedrooms.

If the plane went down and I was stuck on an island, I'd certainly spend my time with him. Probably, he was a womanizer. No, thank you. Or, at the very least, he had a hot girlfriend. A guy like that would have the girls lining up. Heck, I might want to join that line.

I flipped the pages of the book in my hands, but couldn't seem to move my gaze off of the cowboy. Now would be a good time to start reading all about cutting-edge environmental technologies working to limit electromagnetic radiation of cell phone towers in rural areas.

To be honest, it wasn't all that exciting, and most of it was over my head, but if I was going to get the job as an environmental consultant intern, I had to get cracking.

I felt a zing of emotion when I thought of the job. It had to be excitement because it offered the opportunity to take care of myself.

I forced my head down to focus on my electromagnetism book, so I would stop gawking at the male model. As I flipped through my book, searching for my place, a shadow fell over me. I glanced up to find the smiling cowboy entering my aisle.

"Hi." He slid a small suitcase under the seat next to mine.

Mr. Sexy Cowboy was sitting by me. My heart twisted inside my chest. He was just a guy, I told myself as I sucked in my breath. It would be completely embarrassing if he realized my breath had increased to a pant just because he said one word to me.

"Hi," I managed to mutter back.

I couldn't hold eye contact with those beautiful blues, and my face grew warm. I fiddled with the pages of my book, leaning toward the window as he continued to settle in.

He had a rugged, rustic scent that reminded me of the woods I was leaving behind. I pretended to read the blurred type on the page. The back of his hand bumped my thigh as he snapped on his seatbelt. I gasped at the tingle that chased up my leg and spine. He apologized, and his deep voice made my heart skip a beat. He pushed back his cowboy hat on his head, brushing it against the seat.

He removed his hat and dropped it onto his lap, revealing messy dark, thick, curly hair.

My breath caught again.

I needed to make this Cowboy-God something human to allow myself to recover my breath, and so I didn't think about him nonstop for the rest of my life. Attractive guys most often lose their appeal after they became more human.

This cowboy had the power at this moment to stay in my dreams and fantasies for, like, forever.

I cleared my throat and said, "Is Tucson your final destination?"

He glanced out of the corner of his eye, amusement rushing through his face and emphasizing a cute dimple right above his upper lip. "That obvious?" He gestured to his hat and his dark brown, highly decorative boots.

"Not sure." Heat sprang intensely on the back of my neck and across my chest. "I've never been to Tucson before, but I heard somewhere it was country and desert."

His eyebrows raised. "Never been, huh? You'll really like it. You'll find peace and quiet like you won't find anywhere else. Plus, with all the cacti and variety of plants, it is a stunning part of the country." He spoke with a slight southern twang.

Typically, when people assumed what my tastes were, I became upset, but coming from Cowboy-God, it didn't have the same effect. I could be okay with just about anything he said right.

"I'll have to check it out if I get a chance," I said brightly and idiotically.

He grinned.

Everyone settled on the plane, a baby cried softly from up front, and the flight attendant hurried through the cabin for the final check. I watched her quickly go about her job, not wanting to return to my book and not having anything else to say to the cowboy. I was pretty sure my face was some shade of pink or red.

"Planning to stay there long?" His blue eyes caught mine.

I shrugged, not able to look away. He had gentle eyes, the kind a girl would want to gaze into for an extended period of time. "Not sure."

"Well, if you do stay for any amount of time, you'll have to buy a hat." He lifted up his.

I laughed. "I don't think so."

"Why not?"

I shrugged. "I don't look good in them."

He smiled. "I doubt that."

My cheeks grew hot. "Thanks," I muttered.

"Besides," he continued, "it isn't about looks anyway. It is about keeping the sun off your head. Have you ever had a sunburn on your head?"

I laughed. "I don't believe I have."

He grimaced. "You laugh, but I tell you it's not fun at all. Wear a hat if you don't want a painful, scratchy head." He glanced at the flight attendant, who was going through the seatbelt orientation.

When his gaze returned to me, he inclined his head to one side. "So, why Tucson?"

I flushed again. "Job interview. And you?" I quickly added, wanting to shift the subject away from me.

"Race car driver."

He lifted his brows ever so slightly. No doubt waiting for me to ooh and ahh or maybe swoon. I decided not to do either. I wasn't sure how good race cars were on the environment.

"Hmmm," I murmured. "Fancy."

He laughed.

"Do you win?"

His laugh turned into a sultry smile. "All the time."

He quirked an eyebrow in a flirtatious manner, which caused heat to hover between us.

"Hmm," I let the single sound convey skepticism. "To be honest, I'd have guessed cowboy." I nodded toward his hat and gave a quick glance at his outfit.

"I love horses, but I like a couple thousand of them at a time."

That took me a moment, then I got it. I couldn't help a smile easing out with a shake of my head. I conspicuously ruffled the pages of my book as if I was eager to get back to reading.

He watched me a second, then reached for the bag he'd stuffed under the seat.

"What's so great about going fast?" I blurted out.

He paused, mid-bend, then straightened.

I waited for him to rattle off all sorts of manly things about power and control and conquering the mountains or some such, but he didn't say anything at all. Instead, he pushed back in the seat, his long legs hard up against the seat in front of him. Then he tipped his head against the chair and closed his eyes.

Well.

I guess I figured out how to make him human. And a jerk.

I started to open my book when he said very quietly, "Peace."

I looked up. "Pardon?"

He turned to me without lifting his head off the seat. "Going fast is peace. The rest of the world just falls away. There's nothing but you and the track."

I could almost picture the world falling behind as the speed rushed by. He took on a distant gaze as though he was reliving being in the car, zooming down the track. His transfixed expression blended with longing.

He talked about it the way I felt when I was out in nature in Island Park. Me and nature, nothing in-between. Maybe, I sought peace, too, when I stood out there—just me, life, and nothing else. The world disappeared if I stood there long enough, listening and looking. That was a good way of putting it.

"Going fast is a byproduct of trying to outrun the other guy," Ronnie continued after more thought. "From there, everything becomes a technical challenge to do it differently and with various combinations."

I blinked, my skin tingling. "You make it sound like an art form."

"Of course, it is." He shifted in his seat with clear excitement building in him. He leaned closer to me. My heart skipped a beat as I drew closer to him, too, hungry to hear what else he had to say.

"It spews a desire to think outside of the box. Do things differently than everyone else. Doing it, all the same, is boring."

"That's risky."

He smiled, which deepened the lines around his eyes. "Of course. It wouldn't be thrilling if there weren't a real challenge to it."

I stared at his wide eyes. He apparently went after risk. Not to control it. Not to hold back, but to dive in.

"But it could all blow up in your face. Wouldn't that ruin your ranking? You're career?"

He shook his head. "Don't do it for that. It's not about some trophy at the end of the day. It is about living and going for it. A trophy represents a means to an end. The pursuit is the challenge. Diving in and exploring is a lot more satisfying."

He stopped talking, and I stared at this man, waiting for more. He had to have more to say. My patience paid off because, when he saw me waiting and wanting to hear his words, he added, "The technical side of it is fascinating because you end up building your own parts. I get so many ideas on new ways of doing things. Once I retire, I'll dive in on that exploration."

I stared out the window. I understood the love of exploring what was possible. That was how I felt about photography.

"Have you been to a nostalgia drag race event?" The question pulled my attention back to him.

I shook my head. "Can't say I have. I haven't been to any NASA event."

He laughed hard. "You mean, NHRA. The National Hot Rod Association."

I shrugged. "Yeah, that."

He smiled wide, shaking his head. "You've been seriously missing out on life. Haven't been to Tucson or a race car event. Where have you been hiding?"

"Hiding? Idaho, I guess, in snow. With the bears."

"It's time for you to branch out and live a little. Idaho is pretty. There's a racetrack in Boise. It's a five-second track where fast cars run. I have never run there, but it's in the plans. Been there?"

I shifted in my seat as the plane crawled forward. "That's something I didn't know about Idaho. I know about rodeos, horse races, and monster truck shows."

Austin and I traveled to Idaho Falls one weekend to watch a monster truck show. It was dirty. A lot of people were drinking and extremely loud. I had never wanted to go back.

"There's a track in Salt Lake, too," the cowboy continued, intruding into my thoughts. "Was just there today. It's a high altitude, which means we had to change the tune-up on the car to have the car run well. It's still a two-hundred-and-twenty-mile-per-hour track with a nostalgia car. That's what I race. Nostalgia only. I did well today. I ran two-twenty-six."

I blinked, not sure what all that meant other than he was into his tracks and happy about his racing. If he thought my life was boring now, I didn't want to tell him my current job was cleaning houses, and lived with my mommy and her hubby.

"Well, we can't all live in the fast lane." I smiled and then swung my elbow. "Ah, get the pun?"

He smiled again, his dimple coming out. His blues eyes twinkled as he laughed, making him seem like the happiest person on the plane. Maybe the fumes from all that racing had gotten into his head.

Mr. Cowboy shifted in his seat and extended his hand. "I'm Cactus Ronnie Blake, and you are?"

I shook his hand, giving a light laugh, which came out because he made me extremely nervous. His hands were large, rough, tan, and covered with curly black hair. When he touched me with such boldness and determination, my heart skipped another beat. It was sexy, and he was super cute.

"Cactus?"

He laughed. "All racers have nicknames. That's my driver's name. I got it because of my boots and hat."

"I see." I couldn't help raising my eyebrows while suppressing a laugh. "I'm Darlene."

"Darlene, what?"

I flushed. I wasn't sure I wanted to give away my personal information to the good-looking guy I just met sitting next to me on a plane, even if I could swim in those eyes for a very long time. "Just Darlene."

Tipping his chin back, he looked me over. "I get it. I get it. That's okay. You're not comfortable giving your full name to a stranger on a plane. I don't blame you. That's probably wise."

His eyes peered right into mine. Up this close, I could see they were mostly the crystal blue I'd found so startling, but a deep brown outlined the edges of his pupils.

"Tell you what," he continued, "I know we just barely

met, but if you want to come to a race car event and live a little, I'll get you in. I'm racing tomorrow and would love to have you there as my guest."

He put his hand up. "Don't say anything now, just think about it."

Yeah, I'd be thinking about it. Mainly about him, though. Not so much about the racing.

"I will." My voice came out much fainter than intended.

"If you decide that's something you want to do, I'll be at the Tucson Raceway in the far southeast area of town, out about forty miles away from everything."

I nodded like I knew what he was talking about.

"You just call or text me. Do you have paper? I'll write down my number."

He wanted to give me his number. A prickle of excitement jabbed at me. His blue eyes kept gazing at me with such kindness. I decided, this once, I'd take a risk and trust him.

I looked around for something for him to write on, and my gaze landed on my book about magnetism and its effective research for the possible job. Well, that would work.

"Hey, why don't you write it on the last page here." I handed him the book.

"You sure?" He raised his eyebrows and the dimples indented. I presumed this was his trademark look.

I know it was odd to have him write in the book, but I had committed to that, so I stuck to it.

He took the book from me, pulled a pen out of his shirt pocket, wrote down his number, and handed it back.

"Tell you what, if you do call, and want to hang out, I'll

hook you up to do a fire-up."

He was trying to win points with all this, but he had definitely picked the wrong gal because I had no interest in race cars.

"What's a fire-up?" I asked.

He looked me over as his index finger stroked the rim of the cowboy hat in his lap. "You don't even know what a nostalgia funny car is, do you?"

I shrugged. "A funny car. A car that cracks jokes?"

He looked me up and down. "You haven't truly lived if you don't know that. I drive dragsters, but love funny cars, too. Where have you been living all this time?"

"Idaho," I said. "Told you. I live with the bears."

He laughed. "That's cool."

I wasn't sure if it was Idaho or the bears that he found cool, but I did want to know what he was talking about.

"Do you mind me asking? What's a five-second track? Are you saying you only go for five seconds?"

His eyes widened, amazed at my innuendo.

I shuddered from shock at what I had just said.

He took it in stride. "No, the race lasts for about five seconds. Some of the quickest nostalgia funny cars are running five-eighties, five-seventies, which is a very exciting pass."

I brushed my hair off my face. "Well, they don't have five-second anything in Island Park, and that's where I've been hanging out."

"Where's that?" He fingered the brim of his hat.

I looked up at another passenger walking by. "It's about an hour away from Yellowstone National Park. Have you heard of that? Home of Old Faithful?"

"Old Faithful?"

"Have you seen it?" I egged him on. "The natural geyser that shoots off about every forty-five minutes on the clock."

"Don't believe I have," he said.

From the smile on his face, I could tell he knew what I was going to say next. "I guess you haven't really lived either."

He laughed. "I guess I haven't. I'll have to add it to my list. Right now, my whole life is racing. It gets lonely sometimes always on the road or a plane, but I love it." He paused. "Nostalgia racing is reminiscent of the era when drag racing was fun, before big money and politics weaseled into it and transformed the whole sport. Back in the late sixties to the early eighties was a great age of experimentation and design, so no two cars looked alike. Cars you see at NHRA all look the same now and take away the uniqueness of the sport. They zapped the creativity."

I watched this guy who had flipped into lecture mode, and I sensed he knew a lot about this topic.

He inhaled and shook his head slightly, "If you sit in it when I fire it up, you'll hear the thunder, and catch a sense of the power. There isn't anything like it. There are only about three to five hundred cars in the country. It'll be a truly unique experience you aren't likely to forget, I promise."

His energy about the cars made me almost want to see them. If it held this much excitement for him, there must be something to it.

"You sound like a walking advertisement for drag

racing."

That comment made his smile grow even more full. "I probably do."

I looked down at my bag, tucked under the passenger seat in front of me. I wished I knew as much about photography as he knew about drag racing. It'd be cool to just rattle off all the history of the field. "How do you know all this stuff?"

Cactus Ronnie beamed. "I love it. It's my whole life. Ever since I was little, it's all I thought about. My mom even saved the first race car pictures I drew when I was five."

I tried to imagine him at five. Probably thick unruly hair, those big eyes maybe even more innocent, but I bet his intensity was vigorous even then. I could see him clutching a hot rod in his hand like he had a firm grip on his future.

Cactus Ronnie looked a couple of years older than Austin and me, so he was probably in his late twenties. He was set on his career path. Unlike Austin, who was just beginning. And unlike me, who was still exploring. He was fully committed to what he was doing. He didn't have any doubts and wouldn't want to jump ship at the first corporate job offered.

"You're hardcore."

"As hardcore as they come."

My skin prickled as he said this. I found myself leaning toward him, drawn to his energy, his passion. So, I needed to know what hardcore actually meant.

"What does hardcore mean to you?"

He smiled wryly. "It means I eat, breathe, and dream

racing."

My brows furrowed as I imagined this. "You do nothing else?"

"Nope." He shook his head. "I got to do this while I have a chance. I can't let other things get in the way."

I thought about what he said. "That takes commitment."

He nodded. "It does. And sacrifice."

"Is it worth it?"

He didn't respond immediately. It looked like he was giving that some thought. "We shall see, won't we?"

I flushed from his use of "we."

"I don't think I know how it turns out."

He smiled. "I like talking to you. I feel comfortable with you like I can say anything. I like that."

If I hadn't been flushing before, I certainly was now. I could feel the burn on my face. I had never met a person like this guy. I just wanted to hear him ramble on about his passion. There was something so attractive about the way he was all in, simply because it was his thing.

"I like talking to you, too."

His eyes danced.

I needed to watch myself. He was a racer. All I knew about that was some vague concept I must've collected from the movies, and that impression wasn't the kind of guy my mom would want me to hook up with. Actually, *I* probably wouldn't want to hook up with him, either. I wasn't liking the heart-ripped-from-my-chest experience I was having with Austin, and this guy surely attracted a lot of girls. He was too cute and charming not to.

He smiled at me. "I like to keep my life nice and simple. I don't do hard."

I studied him to determine if he was feeding me a line or telling me the truth. He seemed like he was sincere, although I have never heard a person say they don't do hard before.

"But how does that fit with the commitment stuff you talked about?"

A slow smile spread across his face. "I keep my relationships simple, so I can sacrifice for racing. Honoring the time racing requires isn't hard. It's something I do without flinching because it is my passion."

I liked that idea. Maybe I'd adapt that for myself. Maybe that idea could help me figure out where I was going in my life—whatever it was, it shouldn't be hard.

"How did you know what you wanted to do? What to commit to?"

He shrugged. "I know I'm lucky, and it's not like this for everyone, but ever since I saw cars on TV when I was really little, I became enamored with the shape of the car, the colors, the speed. I'd stare at the TV, and the whole world would disappear except me and the cars." He shifted in his seat. "I used to skip school so I could come home and read the racing magazines. It drove my parents crazy. But that was all I wanted to do. I know it's silly, but it sure is a blast."

I sighed, not really able to imagine what that was like. "I wish I knew what I want to do. I want to be that obsessed."

He looked over at me and eyed me up and down. "I was lucky, I know that. But you can figure it out."

The flight attendant loomed above us out of the blue.

He ordered a pop. I ordered water. Maybe a glass of water would cool down my severe attraction to this fascinating man who had his life all figured out. I took the bottle from the smiling blonde woman and sipped. The ice water felt good on my throat.

Cactus Ronnie picked up where our conversation had stopped. "You're on the path right now, taking an adventure and getting out of your comfort zone. That is important."

I certainly wasn't in my comfort zone. My flushing body, mixed with the knots in my stomach, could verify that.

"Talking to me—those are all good steps. All these things will help. Pay attention to what you're passionate about, and you'll figure it out."

That made sense. That made a lot of sense. He said it like it *would* happen. I couldn't help but believe him.

I nodded a few times. "I like that."

He took a sip of his drink and looked at me as though expecting me to say more.

I guess I could open up. "My mom wants me to do school, but I just don't know. She's always talking about having a secure future. She loves me, I know, but I can't think that way."

"Education is always a good thing, but you must follow your passion."

That was a good response, but what was my passion? Was that better than doing what my mom and Austin were doing?

"Are you happy?" I asked.

He smiled wide. "Of course. Happiness comes from following your passion."

I gave that some thought.

His hand came down on the armrest with a thump. "By the way…"

I looked back at him.

He kept his attention on me. "I'm a one-woman type of man. When I do a relationship, I'm loyal."

I shuffled my feet. This conversation had grown really awkward real fast. I shifted in my seat. I guess he could get right to the point, too. But I didn't believe he wasn't a womanizer. That he said it suggested even more that he was. He fit the full formula for a womanizer: attractive, passionate, and charming.

The man had the It Factor. I decided I better respond to his declaration. "That's good to hear."

He shrugged, smiled at me, and settled back in his seat.

Mr. Sexy Cowboy, Cactus Ronnie, and I said nothing more for the last twenty minutes of the flight. My thoughts spun around in my head, thinking about what he'd said. This man was handsome with a capital H, and he claimed he wasn't a womanizer. He was passionate about cars and wore a cowboy hat. I had never met anyone like him.

I don't know why he wasn't talking, but he seemed content to just drink his pop. Or, maybe he had grown tired of chatting. Perhaps his mind was on the upcoming race. I couldn't help but notice how his square jaw gave him an air of certainty and authority. I liked square jaws.

When it came time for us to deplane, he stood, plopped his hat back onto his head, and grabbed his suitcase. "Have a good day, and I hope to hear from you." He turned, leaving me to watch him move confidently down the plane aisle.

CHAPTER 5

*A*t the bottom of the escalator, Austin's smile filled his face as he spotted me. He waved his arms above his head in strong, enthusiastic movements. I uttered a soft wave back. Lots of people stood between him and me, and that was strangely okay.

His brown eyes locked on me with intensity. I looked away. A lump swelled in my throat. Time to return back to reality and kiss the cowboy-racer dream goodbye.

Austin had gone all out, sporting an ocean-blue shirt with jeans. I should be completely mesmerized and happy. This was what I had wanted for a very long time, but thoughts of the cowboy and his crooked smile with the solitary dimple filled my mind, causing me to blush. It was going to be hard to forget that passionate man.

I needed to focus on why I was here, which was to carve out a new life for myself. I needed to leave Idaho and do something important. This job was it, whether Austin and I worked or not.

Guilt flashed through me. Austin and I had agreed to

date other people. All I had done was talk to the cowboy. And, okay, dreamed about what it would be like to kiss a man wearing a cowboy hat. That dream made my whole-body tingle.

I swallowed, remembering the heat that lit me up when I gazed into Cactus Ronnie's eyes. A nervous shiver vibrated in my stomach, and a shy smile snuck onto my lips as I thought of how Ronnie grabbed my book and scrolled his number with confident strokes on the back page. He gave us a way to connect after the flight if I was bold enough to reach out.

The shiver in my stomach turned into a knot. Of course, I wouldn't call. The fact he wanted me to was enough to make me giddy for at least the next week.

I most likely would never see him again…. never see his smile and his natural way of being in this world.

With a lump in my throat, I stepped off the escalator straight into Austin's arms. He held me tight. I leaned away.

He pulled me to him tighter.

I squirmed. He needed to let me go.

The passengers behind me stepped around us, watching like we were the sideshow.

At least I didn't see the cowboy. Hopefully, he had already left.

Before I knew it, Austin started kissing me in front of everyone. I squirmed. He continued to kiss—long and slow. He had never kissed me like that before, even in private.

I pushed against him.

He released me, causing me to stumble back on my feet.

I blinked. "What are you doing?"

He smiled. "Greeting my girlfriend."

I straightened myself, not sure what to do with all the unexpected attention. "You must have missed me," I muttered.

He whispered on top of my head, "I did."

Passengers scurried around us, giving curious stares as though they were wondering what kind of hussy I was. If anyone saw my exchange with the race car driver on the plane, then saw me with Austin, they'd think I was getting around. Maybe they were right. This sucked. I wasn't one of those types of girls, but at this moment, maybe I was.

I tugged my purse strap up higher on my shoulder. Austin's hand found mine, and he pulled on me. "Let's go find your luggage."

Feeling steam wafting off my face, I nodded. I couldn't help giving more darting glances around for the cowboy. My heart was beating rapidly out of my chest, almost hurting. I'd never been any good at cheating on my future spouse. I obviously have no ability to pull off being smooth and quick on my feet.

As we walked, Austin smiled down at me. I had to admit he looked a lot better than the last time I saw him. No longer were their bags under his eyes, and he seemed rested... happy and even confident.

"I'm so glad you're here." He squeezed my fingers. "You're really going to like cell towers."

"Really?" I jogged up to him to match his quick pace.

"They're up to some really cool, environmentally friendly endeavors. They've found scientists who are changing all the eco-unfriendly cell tree towers in India into solar trees that actually work with less impact. The project is completely transforming India. JT has plans to do the same in the United States, and you can be on the team."

Austin had already told me all this before but had probably forgotten with the excitement of traveling. He seemed happy, and if he kept talking, it meant I didn't have to, so I let him ramble on. This job was turning out for him, though it was his trophy, not a passion.

I blinked and forced myself to look at him.

"I'm really starting to fit in. I get along well with the guys. I was the second-best salesman this month."

Austin's eyes had sparkles in them I hadn't seen before. He shone with excitement like he felt alive. Clearly, he was pleased with this new job and path.

Ronnie said the guy in the other lane pushed him down the track, but it wasn't about the trophy for him. The cowboy had that spark, too, but had traveled further down the road than Austin, who was just starting out. Still figuring things out. But there was a clear difference between the two. Creativity and peace motivated Ronnie. For Austin, it was all about the trophy, the opportunity, the money.

Did I want a trophy? Money? Creativity? Peace? Or something completely different?

Austin continued to rattle on until my suitcase arrived, not noticing I wasn't talking back. He grabbed my large pink bag, placed it next to me, and seized me by the waist to pull me firmly against him. He bent down and kissed me again with far more affection than normal.

"I have a surprise for you," he whispered.

I raised my eyebrows, curious but, for some reason, also a bit hesitant. "What is it?"

He gave me the dashing smile that reminded me why I was lucky to be with him. He looked like the boy I had fallen for, with his natural ability to make me feel safe and secure. It was natural being with him.

If I just jumped back into a relationship with him, I could be forever fighting against his attention and loyalty to his mom, and living in Tucson working for a cell tower company. All that, without knowing if it was what I really wanted.

Being with Austin defined my life in a box. I didn't even know what that box looked like. I needed to take my time to figure out the box dimensions and requirements, so I understood what I was climbing into and how to be safe.

He squeezed my hand, excited about the surprise he had for me. "You'll have to wait until we're in the car. Do you think you can wait that long?"

He wanted to play. We used to be light and bantering all the time, and now he wanted to go back there even though we both knew we couldn't. Surprisingly, I wasn't even sure I wanted to.

Maybe he really was happy because of his work. Maybe, Jackson was right that men needed a good job to be their best selves. Maybe I needed a different job too to find that same kind of happiness for myself.

A bright glare of sunlight slipping in from the glass exit doors hit my eyes. I squinted. I could play. "No." I tugged on his arm. "Tell me now."

The sliding door opened, letting in a gentle breeze. He knew I was never one to wait to find out about a surprise.

He laughed, liking the power he had over me. His mouth settled into a smirk. "Not going to."

He wanted me to beg, and I didn't have the strength to fight it, so I gave him what he wanted. I headed toward the parking lot, holding his one hand while he toted my suitcase with the other. I huffed along, lugging my overstuffed carry-on with all my camera equipment.

"Please, tell me what it is."

"Nope." He took my carry-on from me.

"Hint?" I asked, relieved to no longer carry my bag.

His jaw tightened as he shook his head.

He certainly was acting secretive. I couldn't imagine what he was up to. He had never gotten me something before when he went away. I continued to ask him what it was, but he wouldn't say anything.

When we finally loaded into the parked car and snapped into our seatbelts, he said, "Here you go." He flopped something wrapped in a plastic supermarket bag onto my lap. It was about the size of a small cat.

His brown eyes earnestly watched me. My stomach quivered, not sure what he was up to. "What is this?"

He nodded toward it. "Open it and find out."

He was coming on too strong with all the kisses, the hugs, constant touching, and now getting me a gift. I blew out a deep breath, not liking the pressure that threatened to take me over.

I shifted in my seat. This situation felt fake, like a family picture where everyone is plastering on smiles that don't even look real. I didn't want fake. Or pressure. I wanted to go back to when I wasn't thinking about moving, and my career, and school, and the cowboy on the plane.

The heaviness of the gift rested on my legs. I picked it up and the plastic bag crinkled in my hands. I shook it.

Austin placed a hand on top of mine. "Be careful."

"Must be breakable," I muttered. The plastic bag crinkled louder as I began to unwrap it, sweating. The car was hot and muggy, and I was regretting wearing jeans and a cotton mid-sleeve shirt with a collar and buttons. It was far too hot for this kind of weather.

I stopped unwrapping. "Would you mind putting on the air conditioning? It's really hot here."

I tugged hard on the extra-strong tape as Austin started the car.

Finally, I unfolded the plastic bag enough to see the latest model camera. It tumbled out of the bag, and I read through the features. It offered a lot more options than my old camera.

I loved it. I absolutely loved it.

I looked up to Austin, who wore a soft smile. "Thank you."

"I remembered how much you loved to take pictures of flowers when we first met." He spoke softly.

I had loved taking those pictures. I had gone crazy with all the wildflowers and was always on the lookout for the next photo. "I remember you complaining obsessively every time I wanted us to pull over to take a picture."

Austin shifted the car into reverse. "I hope you like it. It's something fun you can do as a hobby."

I bristled at the word "hobby." Of course, that was what it was, but him calling it that bothered me. Shaking it off, I reached out and caressed his bristly chin. "I love it. Thank you. This was very nice of you."

He smiled, pecked me on the lips, and then moved to sit straight in his seat. "We need to get out of here. JT will be waiting for us."

I thoroughly read the back of the package to see all its new features as we left the small airport. Soon, we were on the road so bumpy my teeth rattled, and I could no longer clearly see the writing on the box.

I stared out at this place that both Austin and the cowboy had described. The air conditioning in the car struggled to compete with the thick heat. I wiped at my face. It was hot. It looked hot outside. It looked as hot as it felt.

"Can we stop the car for a second?" I asked.

"We need to get you to your interview."

I stared at the long thin cactus that branched up with arms reaching for the pale blue sky. There were so many angles I could use to play with that frame. "I want to take pictures of this place. I want to see if I can capture the heat."

"Maybe later."

"But it'll cool down," I whined.

"Not much," he muttered.

Out the window, I was greeted by old houses in light shades of pink, tan, and purple lining the road, giving the area a dated feel. None of the places had green grass.

"Could you at least slow down so I can get some of those old houses? I want to capture the purple one."

"Not now."

I slumped back into my seat. Most of the houses had colorless rocks in front and rusty old cars parked along the sides left over from the '50s. It gave me an image of being frozen in time.

A few miles later, we neared a run-down, old cafe, just like the ones seen on any street in small-town America.

Austin reached over and squeezed my hand. "Hungry? We could run through a hamburger joint and then straight to JT's."

With the mere mention of Mr. Devonshire, I remembered I was supposed to be having my first interview for a job ever. My stomach tightened as the car cooled. I started to feel ill.

"Oh, crap. An interview. I almost forgot about everything."

Austin looked at me. "You'll do great."

I doubted that, but I didn't want to talk about it. "A hamburger sounds good," I said as my stomach rumbled.

"I'll change at the restaurant then." I reached out with my right hand and gripped the armrest. "So, how's your mom?"

It may have been a mistake bringing her up, but it might give me an idea of what kind of life Austin had recreated for himself here.

"She's fine," Austin said. His voice strained. "She's throwing a party for work at JT's house tonight for all the employees. They just barely refinished his kitchen, and she's ordering in food. They've hired a live band, so it's going to be real cool."

My throat tightened, and it had become hard to eat. "Let me guess... you want me to go with you?"

Austin looked over at me with raised eyebrows. "Of course!"

The knots in my stomach increased. I didn't even know if I could get the job. I didn't know if I wanted the job. I didn't know where I stood with Austin or where he stood with me. I didn't even know anything about this strange town that looked so different from Idaho, and he wanted me to go to an office party for my one night here?

"Can't we do something else? I haven't seen you for weeks. I miss you. I want time together. We haven't even caught up."

He squeezed my hand. "I know. But this is the time for you to meet everyone you'll be working with."

My heart picked up its pounding. He was assuming a lot of things with that statement. First, that I'd secure the job, which wasn't a given. Second, I'd take the job, which again wasn't a given, even though I pretty much suspected I'd take it. Especially if it really could help improve the environment. Third, I did need to get away from my parents. Fourth, I wanted to get to know who I was working with. I have been working by myself for basically a really long time. And the fifth reason, I wasn't going to tell him... I might want to slip away and go to the race track instead. My heart picked up speed with that thought.

Cactus Ronnie's invitation was calling me in a big way. I just wanted to look into his stunning blue eyes one more time and maybe see him at work. If a man talked about his work the way he talked about his, it must be *something* to watch him actually do his job.

And if I was going to be completely honest, I couldn't get the thought of kissing him out of my mind. I just wanted to know what it was like.

* * *

MY STOMACH HAD GONE from clenching to double clenching as we made our way across the very large town. This job interview was my chance to get out of Island Park, be out on my own, and actually do something important in helping Mother Earth.

My hand circled around my new camera. It'd be cool to do something like that. I stared at the long highway in front of us. It had a lot more cars than I had ever seen in Idaho. Everything was so different here.

Austin ordered me a hamburger and fries through a drive-thru. Five minutes later, a greasy bag sat on my lap. I took a bite of two fries but didn't make it through the second fry. Instead, I slipped it back into the bag.

"Aren't you going to eat that?" Austin asked.

"Can't," I muttered.

He shrugged. "Mind if I have it then?"

I plopped my bag of food onto the console between us. "Be my guest."

It took him a matter of seconds to down the entire meal before he proceeded onto his own. His appetite hadn't changed, but his hair had gotten longer with more waves, which made him look more preppy, more stylish, and, honestly, cuter. He had also gotten tanner and might have put on a pound or two of muscle. I swallowed a lump in my throat. Couldn't anything stay the same?

The intensity of the sun muted any colors from surfacing for miles. Drab stores and small houses shrank from its blazing rays. Saguaro cacti stood boldly, withstanding the heat with their green prickly arms reaching toward the sky in defiance, declaring their hearty, long-lived natures. The rest of the country was buried under the snow, making this place a mysterious town despite its muted color scheme.

Austin continued to talk about work, the town, and life in general as we neared the warehouse where my interview would take place. The houses had grown smaller in size and were more spread out.

A lot of flat land continued on forever, occupied by cacti and weeds. In its own way, this empty land held its own beauty. It might be fun to spend time wandering around to discover what sights the camera might find.

In the near distance off to one side of the freeway, a parking lot of planes caught my attention. They looked like they were used in one of the world wars. Thirty or forty planes just sat there like someone forgot they left them there. Hopefully, someone would figure out what to do with them soon.

"You really like it here?" I asked.

Austin nodded. "People say it's hot, but I really haven't found it too bad. It's so pretty. I love the variety of greens."

I looked back out the window. He had to be kidding but, apparently, he wasn't. Greens? Not too hot? I was still dealing with the heat the air conditioning couldn't handle.

Five minutes later, we pulled up to a large warehouse with, at least, nine-foot-tall wire fences surrounding it, like a prison.

Austin smiled at me, and I gulped a lump down, trying to remind myself I didn't have to take the job. I didn't have to impress this man, and I didn't have to leave the truly beautiful state of Idaho to live in this desolate place where people wore cowboy hats even more often than they did in Idaho. I could live with my parents forever, keep things the same… Well, without Austin. I could do that. I could. Did I want to?

"You'll do great." Austin looked over at me before taking the key out of the ignition.

He grabbed a napkin and wiped his hands from his meal, then opened my car door.

The nervous dancing in my stomach switched onto overload. I climbed out of the car and straightened the skirt my mom helped me pick out to look professional. I wobbled a bit in the high heels, not used to wearing them. Maybe I hadn't worn them since high school prom, which was quickly becoming a distant memory.

Out of the usual sweats and T-shirts I wore to clean, I felt like I was playing dress-up.

Cactus Ronnie said on the flight that simply taking a plane to come here was moving me closer to my passion. I hoped he was right. Maybe this interview would give me a clue if I was on the right path. That would be nice.

Austin took me into a dark room lit by an overhead fluorescent light, with open metal folding chairs and a folding table. He wasn't holding my hand, which I was glad about. Time for me to play the part of a professional. Suddenly, I was trying on adult shoes to walk into my new life. I wobbled in the attempt like wearing high heels for the first time.

Austin gestured for me to sit. "I'll be back soon."

I sat on a metal chair and took deep breaths as I looked at the cement walls sporting a few cheesy posters taped on them. This company wasn't going for aesthetics.

It didn't take long for Austin to return with a tall, clean-shaven, older man. He wore cowboy boots and an air of commanding authority.

He gave me one look and forced a smile. "You must be Darlene." He extended his hand. "JT."

We shook hands, and he guided me to the back of the office to his office. It held a nice wooden desk, luxurious but comfortable chairs, and a couch. This appeared more like what I thought I'd find.

I took the side corner of a couch and curled up next to the armrest. Austin sat firmly in the middle of the couch next to me, taking up a lot more space. He and Mr. Devonshire did a lot of talking about updating certain checklists, then JT moved his focus to me.

I swallowed the reoccurring lump in my throat, convinced I wouldn't remember any facts I had read in the airport to prepare for this meeting. Mr. Devonshire was an attractive older man who stared at me with a tight jaw and eyes narrowed just enough to make me more nervous.

"What's your schooling?"

My eyes shifted to the coffee table, and I stared at the glossy wooden surface. With a mother as a former university professor, I should've been ashamed of my education status, but I never had been—until now.

"High school." My voice cracked. My chest pounded. I needed to be more confident.

"No college courses?"

"No, sir. Not yet. I've been busy cleaning cabins. Um, my job right now. It keeps me busy."

The questions didn't get any better as I muddled my way through the interview. I could tell by the increased pout in the lines around JT's mouth he wasn't too impressed. Despite what Austin wanted, I wasn't going to get the job.

This man was looking for someone good with science, who had an understanding of all these systems, and who could apply these principles into the workplace. I had none of that.

When it was over, JT stood and shook my hand. "We'll be in touch." He glanced at his watch. "I've another meeting to get to. It was nice to meet you."

Austin smiled brightly, as though he hadn't just witnessed me take a massive nosedive.

"See you tonight, sir," he said.

By the time the gravel crunched under our feet as Austin escorted me back to the car, my heart pounded hard with the sense of failure. I might not ever make it out of cleaning cabins.

Before the interview, that work had been good enough for me. Right now, it felt limiting. I thought of Cactus Ronnie and how alive he was with his work and how excited. In fact, Austin seemed to be that way, too, in his own way. A heaviness pressed down on me. Would I ever get like that? Would I ever be able to find my own way?

"I didn't get it," I whispered.

"What?" Austin stopped walking and peered at me with another surprised expression. "Of course you did."

I shook my head with certainty. "No, he wasn't happy about my lack of education. I don't have the skills he was looking for. Didn't you see how many times he frowned?"

Austin flipped his keys in his hands and continued on to the car. "Naw, I doubt that matters. He hired me, and he knows I don't have a college degree, either. I'm sure you'll be fine."

"You're Maggie's kid, and I'm not," I said. I pressed my lips together. I shouldn't have said that. I shouldn't be tearing him down because I didn't make it.

"That doesn't have anything to do with it."

Austin unlocked the doors for both of us.

We climbed into the car. "Of course, it does." I wanted to say more, but it would have just caused a fight, and I didn't want that. Austin had to know he was getting a break because of his mom. It was fine. She had caused him a lot of pain in the past by stealing his college money. She owed him that much, but the rest of us weren't in the same situation.

Austin cleared his throat, which broke into my thoughts. "I'm going to take you to the hotel. Can you stay there for a couple of hours? I have work I need to do, then we have a party to get to."

The car fell silent. What was there to say? I was at his beck and call since I was the one visiting. I didn't have a car or know anyone except Cactus Ronnie, and knowing a drag-car racer at a strip at least forty miles away probably wasn't going to help.

Anyway, I didn't "know" him, I reminded myself. No matter how much it felt like we connected on the phone. It was a fly-by, literally. I'd never seen him again. Time to move on with real life.

"Sure, No problem. I'll just... you know, hang around." I hoped I sounded braver than I felt.

"You can play with your camera or go swimming," Austin suggested.

He was trying to be helpful, but those comments crawled under my skin. He was acting like I couldn't figure out what to do on my own. I didn't want to be told what to do. I wanted to be heard about what I just said about the job. I wanted him to understand I was embarrassed and to somehow make it better. That was unrealistic but, even so, he wasn't getting me at all.

Cactus Ronnie had seemed to understand more of me than Austin did.

Forget about the race car driver. I told myself sternly.

My focus now was on real life. Austin. Corporate America. Cell phone towers. Maybe. If I got the job. And if not...

Heat dripped down my chest. I reached for my new camera and held it tight on my lap as we drove forward in silence surrounded by cactus and dirt.

"I'll be fine," I said. "I'll take some pictures."

CHAPTER 6

This was my first time to see the other side of the mountain. And here I was, alone, confined to a small ugly dark hotel room that smelled of mold. The room sported a very nasty, worn-out orange and dark-brown bedspread.

Austin waved good-bye to me on his way back to work. The door snapped shut behind him, leaving me there to rot.

I tossed my bag on the wooden chair and blinked into the darkness. Austin hadn't kissed me goodbye. Instead, he suggested I take a nap. I looked at the multi-colored remnant from the Seventies covering the bed and wondered how many bedbugs must be crawling on it. Napping wasn't going to happen.

I strolled to the window and peeked out at the great view of the hotel trash bin. A few old rusty cars dotted the parking lot along with some stunted cacti whose arms reached toward the sky. Cactus was something I didn't see every day.

Camera shooting time!

Five minutes later, I closed my hotel room door behind me with a thud, ready to explore this whole new world through my new camera lens. I looked down the hall with all of its closed doors. A line of matching doorknobs provided a hint of something lurking behind them.

I pulled up my camera and pressed my body into the doorframe. I squatted down until all the lines of the door-knobs filled the frame. I took a minute to figure out the settings needed to make the camera create an off-focus shot and snapped.

* * *

HOURS LATER, I wandered back into the hotel's entryway covered in sweat. I needed ice-cold water, but that didn't stop my excitement from having a camera of interesting pictures to sort through.

A stand next to the front desk of the hotel held a jug of cool water with orange slices floating in it. I hurried over and filled a plastic cup with ice water. I had completely drunk one glass of water and was about to pour another when I noticed a poster hanging behind the jug.

The poster showed race cars—the long narrow kind. Curious, I crept closer to see the super-sexy Cactus Ronnie smiling back at me. Just seeing him with that extra cute, flirtatious smile made me catch my breath. The photographer had done a good job of capturing his charm.

The poster declared him a local hero, who would tear up the racetrack tonight. Just like he told me on the plane.

I faced the poster head-on and admired how Ronnie

smiled into the camera in the same natural way he had when he plopped down next to me on the airplane. I gazed into his blue eyes but stopped myself.

He wasn't real life. I needed to forget about him.

He offered to show me around the races tonight. My heart fluttered. That would be something.

"There you are!"

I turned to see Austin, brows furrowed. "Where have you been? Why weren't you in your room?"

I gestured to my camera. "Taking pictures."

He brushed that aside. "Ready to go?"

"What?"

"The party."

I blinked at him. There was my harsh re-entrance into reality.

* * *

I TOOK A QUICK SHOWER, and thirty-five minutes later, we pulled up to what looked like a rancher's mansion. Cows nibbled on the brown grass, and a wire fence followed the dirt road up to the house. That would make a good picture with the setting sun later. It also might be fun to see what my camera did with cows if I took a picture of them in the dark. Would anything show?

Austin smiled at me. "Thanks for coming."

I nodded, remembering it was time for me to be a good girlfriend. Part of that involved dealing with his vain mother. I pulled my camera closer, needing all the strength I could muster. It had been a long time since I had to deal with her and, truthfully, I'd rather not.

It didn't take long for Austin to open up my car door onto the hot warmth of the fading day.

Since I bombed the interview, I wouldn't have to worry about moving here. I glanced back at the cows. I needed to take advantage of photographing this place tonight.

I could do a whole collection of cows. Cows from Idaho and Arizona. Revealing the differences in sunlight, vegetation, and, somehow, I hoped to capture the temperature in those shots, too.

The houses represented the heat quite well... all flat and spread out, as though shrinking from the sun. These flat-roofed homes hugged the earth, making them look unsure if they could otherwise survive. They were like me. I wasn't sure I could withstand the heat of figuring out my life.

Austin grabbed my hand as we weaved around red and black sports cars already parked in front of the house. He strolled toward the side door and opened it for me to go in.

I hesitated to step in. I stared at the floor, shrinking from doing this like the houses shrank from the sun. Maybe we could keep this short and spend our last night together doing something more fun.

I squeezed Austin's hand before stepping into the house full of adults buzzing with talk. Almost everyone wore shorts, tanks, and sandals with a glass of wine in their hands. Chips, salsa, chopped up broccoli, and cauliflower filled the kitchen countertop.

Despite all the commotion, my eyes zeroed in on one person. Maggie. Her hair was still silky blonde, her makeup caked on, and she wore a shiny, short, green dress.

She looked up at us and stopped chopping vegetables. My hand tightened around Austin's.

A broad smile spread across her face. "Baby, you made it."

She wiped her hands on her apron before scurrying over to put her hands on Austin's face. "Oh, you're so cute."

She kissed him on both cheeks, then returned to cutting her carrots.

"Hi, Mrs. Chambers." My voice didn't come out as strong and steady as I wanted it to.

Maggie brushed a long strand of hair off her shoulder as a flicker of irritation crossed her face. She quickly masked it and looked back to Austin. "How's the deal with McCoughal going?"

I gripped tighter onto Austin's hand. He squeezed my fingers back. She was acting like I wasn't even here. Completely ignoring me.

"We had a meeting with them this afternoon." Austin grabbed a small flower of broccoli and plopped it into his mouth. "It looks promising."

I cleared my throat.

Austin peered down at me. "Want some food? There's a plate over there."

I ignored that. Broccoli and cauliflower weren't the answer. I expected Austin to stand up for me in front of his mom but, instead, he turned his attention back to her.

"They want JT to flesh out more ideas before our meeting tomorrow morning, so he might be a little later than you thought."

Austin grabbed a handful of chips.

Maggie shrugged. "That seems to happen a lot lately. But the possibilities they're creating are exciting."

Austin shoved the handful of chips into his mouth, causing crumbs to spill onto the floor and counter.

With the side edge of a knife, Maggie brushed a pile of cauliflower onto the vegetable tray. "Did I tell you…"

And off went Austin and his mom, without further acknowledgment of my presence.

I stood there trying to think about what to do to make the situation better, but all I could think about was the cow in the twilight. I really wanted to get that shot.

Austin continued eating, and Maggie continued chopping as they talked about work. This wasn't going to stop anytime soon, and the sun would sneak behind the horizon within the next few hours.

I whispered to Austin, "I'll be back in a minute."

"What?" A line deepened near his lips.

"I'm taking pictures of the cow. I'll be back."

He nodded like he heard me, but I could tell he hadn't. Mom took all his focus.

I pulled away from him and slipped outside. I hiked over the wire fence and started snapping pictures of the cows in the distance.

My eyes stayed focused on one large animal in case it decided it wanted to act like a bull instead of a cow and charge me. The heat of the evening wrapped around me less intensely than it had a couple of hours ago.

As I took pictures, motorcycles sped in, ridden by middle-aged men, who climbed off their bikes, slapped each other on the shoulders, and streamed into the kitchen. Another reminder of how I didn't belong here in the yard.

The cows didn't flinch, but I took it as a sign I needed

to head back inside. Dirt covered my shoes, but I chose to ignore that as I walked up to Austin. It was time to show him I could be a good girlfriend.

He was talking to the motorcyclists gathering food onto plates. I stood by his side so they'd know I was with him. He gave a quick glance at me and took my hand, but as people joined his circle, he stepped up shoulder-to-shoulder with the men. That more-or-less edged me out. I stood holding his hand but wasn't able to look at anyone he talked to.

I gazed out the window seeing various cacti towering over the dirt and wild green plants. The sunlight had already shifted again.

Tucson was a mystery, and taking the plane an adventure, but now I was assigned to sit in the corner munching on chips all night. Why did I decide to give up the races for this one night I was in town, just to sit here, ignored, at an office party I didn't belong to?

My heart thudded.

I could see Cactus Ronnie if I wanted. Just for one night. He was a phone call away.

I wasn't moving to Tucson. This was my one night to explore the other side of the mountain. This might be my only chance to explore.

I let go of Austin's hand. He didn't notice.

"Austin?"

He ignored me and added a comment, which set the group around him to chuckling.

Time to make a couple of phone calls.

CHAPTER 7

*T*wenty minutes later, I sat in a taxi, confirming the address to the racetrack with the quiet foreign driver. I hoped the driver didn't turn out to be an ax murderer like in the horror films.

I wiped the sweat from my palms onto my pant leg and took a deep breath before peering back at the party. Guilt poked at me. It was rude to just take off like this. I should tell Austin where I was going. I looked at the house, thinking about doing it…

Nope. Couldn't.

I admitted it. I was a chicken, especially with Maggie around. I didn't want to make a big scene. I just wanted to see what a racetrack was like and, okay, maybe see Cactus Ronnie's smile one more time. Besides, Austin was the one who left for the big fancy job. He was the one ignoring me at the party. He was the one moving on.

That didn't change the fact it was rude for me to disappear. I looked at my phone. Nothing. Austin hadn't even noticed I had left. I was going to have to apologize

93

for this. If I told him where I was going, he'd try to stop me and might be mad at me for interrupting his schmoozing.

Just this one night... just this one adventure. I'd make it up to him somehow. I held my camera close to me. He'd forgive me for this. I was pretty sure he would.

"Good evening." The taxi driver brought my attention back to what I was doing... sneaking out of a party.

My fingers tightened around my camera case. I was doing this. Seriously, if Mom knew I had caught a taxi and traveled out to a racetrack to see a stranger I met on a plane, she'd skin me alive. She'd first tell me a full history of race car superstitions. She'd be full of advice, like not to go anywhere near a green race car, etc.

Cactus Ronnie had been more than welcoming on the call, even though it was hard to hear with engines blasting off in the background.

"Darlene, from the plane. So you want to see the races?" he asked.

I forced myself to find at least one word. "Yes."

"Do you have a car?"

My breath picked up speed. I had forgotten about that part. Of course, he was at the track and wouldn't be able to get me. Feeling stupid, I said, "No." Heat crawled up my neck.

Loud thundering noises ate into the phone line. "Text me your address and I'll have a taxi pick you up. I'll have a pass waiting for you at the front gate. I'm glad you called. You're going to have a great time."

More roaring on the phone.

"See you soon." He hung up.

Two minutes later, a text with the taxi information clicked in with more information about retrieving the pass.

I blinked at the phone. That had been easy.

Later, while the taxi driver programmed the address of the racetrack into his GPS, I gazed at the large rambling house and the lines of expensive BMWs and Lexuses parked along its drive. I should say goodbye to Austin, but the taxi started slowly back out to the street. Besides, Cactus Ronnie was waiting for me.

"Lots of traffic tonight?" I asked the cab driver.

"No, it's fairly light. We aren't plagued with the snow-birds yet."

I nodded, with guilt still sitting in my stomach like a dead weight. I'd made the call a half-hour ago, and he still hadn't noticed.

Anger thumped through me, causing my temperature to rise. The taxi wasn't overly hot, but it wasn't a pleasant temperature either. I had flown all the way out here to be with Austin, and he didn't even notice I was gone? I didn't need all his attention, but a little, like noticing I wasn't even at the party, would be nice.

The taxi hit a pothole, jolting my attention back to the road. "It's bumpy."

The taxi driver nodded with an energetic agreement. "This city is famous for its potholes. All the money goes to the bicyclists and none to the roads. It's a real racket, I tell ya."

Austin knew I felt uncomfortable at parties. He knew his mom didn't like me. He knew I didn't know anyone there and he still forgot about me.

The taxi crawled to a stop for a light.

It was too late now. I was on my way to a racetrack to see a man I had just met on a plane. A man with the nickname, "Cactus." My throat abruptly tightened, and my heart pounded. What was I doing? I never did impulsive things like this. This wasn't a safe, predictable thing to do.

I closed my eyes to settle myself down. Anger continued to burn in my chest. I wanted to see just how long it'd take Austin to find out I took off. That wasn't mature, but I was curious just how much he wasn't thinking about me.

I fingered my camera, then stared at the blank screen of my phone. No missed phone call, no text, no anything. I'd tell Austin I had decided to do something else after he texted or called and wait for him to reach out.

The sun slipped down toward the earth as the taxi drove on a road that loomed straight into forever. My nerves knocked around in my chest. I had to focus on steadying my breath, so the driver didn't think there was something wrong.

For a while, we drove through town, but a right turn took us down another long straight road that passed shopping centers, housing centers, and lots and lot of land. Land that wanted my camera to take pictures of it.

Eventually, the driver made another turn onto a dirt road where billows of dust followed us. Before I knew it, the dirt road ended in a large flat patch of pavement. In some semblance of rows, cars, trucks, and motorcycles parked—both inside and out of an entrance gate.

This was it. A car racetrack. My neck tightened. Lots of people carried plastic cups full of beer, wandered in every direction, and talked in excited voices. All were dressed for a fair in shorts, old blue jeans, and cowboy hats in reds, blues, browns, blacks, and pinks. A misting of the crowd sported heavy metal band T-shirts.

I dug into my purse to find my cash. I thanked the cab driver and handed him the fare with a tip.

He took it and peered over the vast car landscape. "Do you want me to pull up closer?"

"No." I undid my seatbelt. "I'm good," I said with far more confidence than I felt.

The taxi driver gave me a nod. I closed my door, and he waved as he drove away. I watched the dust follow his car. He was going to have to wash that car tomorrow.

I turned around to face a fairground now transformed into a racing venue. A fence circled, for what seemed like miles, around the track, stadium, and car pits. Large yellow overhead lights glared in the distance, highlighting the cars. Noise in the background swarmed the place with a roar of speeding cars tearing forward. As yet unseen, they were over there somewhere scrapping for fame and records.

In the midst of this, over a PA system, a male announcer's voice yelled the feats accomplished. Clusters of talking visitors reacted with animated enthusiasm.

Smells of greasy foods, dust, beer, and an occasional whiff of wine drifted past me. I inhaled it all in. I had never seen a place so brimming with life, other than early morning in Yellowstone. Especially at the beginning of spring when the flowers woke along with the hibernating bears, the driven salmon, and the young birds testing out their wings.

I let the frenzy seep in as I tried to figure out how to

find Cactus Ronnie. He had said there would be a ticket waiting at the front booth on the west side entrance. That was all good and dandy, but I had no idea which way was west, nor could I see any "booth."

I hustled to the fence, trying to ignore the rapid pulse beating in my throat as a long line of people, cars, trucks, and motorcycles streamed into the racetrack fairgrounds. I wiped sweat onto the front of my jeans.

How was I supposed to find Cactus Ronnie?

Tears pressed against my eyes. "I can handle this," I whispered. I told my parents I'd be fine. And I would be fine. I just needed to find the booth. Or, at least, figure out which way was west. Maybe I should have asked the taxi driver? He would have known. I turned to see his car's settling dust.

Shoulders slumped, I thought about how else to figure this out. Everyone seemed to be funneling into one gate, some flashing wristbands at the security guards, others with stamps on their hands. Beyond the gatekeepers stood a colossal metal grandstand like I'd seen in photos of ballparks.

Loud roars thundered.

Among the hundreds of people, I tucked my camera closer to my torso, but stopped walking to take in all the colors of the event, people, cars, and lights. This was too good to miss.

I held the camera up to capture the overhead lights spilling down their yellow glow onto the track. But the camera also captured distant cacti, dark rolling purple mountains, and the brightness of a quarter moon to declare the timelessness always around us.

I let everything flow and rush around me as I absorbed the sight, the moment. I snapped one picture, then another, and stepped back to play with space. I may never again have another chance to grab this exact image.

The sky was dusted with the descending hues of light blue as a subtle accent. Distant white clouds lumbered over the blue, crawling over the sky toward night. They provided the needed contrast to avoid drab and create brilliance.

The mountains had faded into a royal purple to display their stature for all who cared to look. The sky, clouds, stadium, and overhead lights enchanted me.

My peek into this completely different world promised many surprises. It swarmed with the noises of activity, so different from the miles upon miles of wilderness in the Rockies.

I hunted for clues as to where I was supposed to go for tickets, pacing up and down the fence in the toasty heat that hadn't lessened much with the lowering of the sun. Nothing looked like a booth that held a ticket with my name on it.

Panic settled in the pit of my stomach. Maybe I shouldn't do this. Maybe I should call the taxi back and see if I could make it to Maggie's party before anyone noticed. I stopped walking for a second to look at my phone screen to see if Austin had reached out yet.

He hadn't.

My hands shook. I had to do something. I couldn't stand out here by myself, and I wasn't sure if I had enough money to get back to my hotel room. With no choice left, I had to call Ronnie.

I took a deep breath before I dialed. My heart thundered in my chest. He was going to think I was a ditz for not being able to find the ticket office.

"You here?" His voice sounded comforting and exciting.

"Lost."

He laughed hard. "Okay, where you at? I'll come to get you."

Goosebumps chased up my arm. He sounded as delighted to see me as I was him.

"Okay." I heard the shyness in my tone of voice. I was definitely out of flirting practice.

He was, after all, a stranger, and running off to meet him was not a smart thing to do, especially in a town where the only one who knew me was Austin. And he certainly wasn't going to be reachable anytime soon.

"Where are you?" Cactus Ronnie's voice pierced through my panic.

Even though he couldn't see me, I shrugged. "Um-m," I said, looking around for some signpost marker I could give him. "In the parking lot with a lot of cars and stuff outside the gate." I hurried to the fence that wrapped around the grounds so I could be more precise on my location. "I see a sign that says Gate C."

"Oh, that's way out there. Okay, that's fine. Start walking west, and I'll head toward you right now as we speak."

I shuffled my feet. "Um, which way is west?"

He laughed again. I was glad he found me being lost amusing. "Away from the mountains."

Bluish purple mountains were in every direction.

Maybe he meant the closest to me. "Okay, I think I'm going the right way."

Cactus Ronnie said something to someone else about coming back.

"Don't worry. I'll find you," he said to me.

That was comforting. I wanted to be found. I had been feeling lost lately, stuck in an isolated wilderness with Austin gone. It'd be really nice to be found. I weaved through lots of people.

My heart beat faster than the roar of the race car engines in the background. This had to be absolutely the craziest thing I have ever done. Hands down the craziest and, so far, I was loving it.

Just as confusion and fear began to make my hands tremble again, I glanced up to see a tall, slender race-car driver with the familiar cowboy hat strutting toward me with a big smile. He strolled right up, wrapped his arms around me, and gave me a tight hug. "I'm glad you came." He squeezed my shoulders and peered down at me, sweeping me up into his blue gaze.

This man took my breath. I stood there staring at him, not talking for at least twenty seconds. My brain kept telling me to *say something*, but I couldn't. I just stood there flushed and smiling… for sure looking like a dork.

"Come on. I'm going to be up soon." He grabbed my hand and, before I knew it, an entrance bracelet was slapped on my wrist, and I found myself hurrying down the pavement headed toward the racetrack.

We squeezed through a narrow space, passing a lot of cars with long noses and huge wheels. Thin people sat in the cars with helmets on or stood just outside the narrow metal-framed race cars, jawboning.

"Hey, Cactus," called out one of the guys standing by a race car with a shorter nose than the others. The car was drowned in royal blue with curly white writing on it. "Who's with you?"

A smile crossed Cactus Ronnie's face. "This is Darlene. Darlene, I'd like you to meet Road Crusher. He's a legendary racer from back in the day. He won a lot of races."

I smiled at him. "Hi."

He winked. "I only won the important races." He extended his tan, calloused hand.

I shook it.

"What are you doing, hanging out with a shady creature like this?" He thumbed toward Cactus Ronnie.

I shrugged, ready to play this game with these guys. Clearly, they were fond of each other. "Not sure."

The older man burst out in laughter. "She's a keeper."

Cactus Ronnie tilted his cowboy hat further back on his head. "This is Darlene's first exposure to nitro cars."

The older gentleman looked at me with inquisitive eyes and with a hint of disbelief. "Really? You're going to love it. All it takes is one drink of the nitro fumes, and you'll be hooked." He leaned in closer to me as though telling me a secret. "There's nothing like it. Once you're washed in it, you'll do anything to drink it again."

Drink of nitro fumes?

"Nitro?" I asked.

"Nitromethane, a monopropellant, which means it carries an oxygen atom," Ronnie said.

I had no idea what that meant, and it must've shown on my face because Road Cruncher added, "It's the reason it makes so much horsepower."

Ronnie nodded like Road Cruncher had given the correct answer. "The engine breathes it as a fuel, and, as it does, it adds oxygen to the engine."

Road Cruncher leaned over to me again like a conspirator and whispered, "It can be used as rocket fuel."

"Lousy rocket fuel." Ronnie shook his head.

Either way, it sounded dangerous. These guys talked like they were addicted, and nitro was the best thing in the world.

Deafening cars ate pavement and thundered in the background. The wails of piercing noises made my ears ring. I loved experiencing the liveliness, the excitement in the air. I could almost reach out and take handfuls to taste.

Some of the people who had been walking past us had on headsets to block the noise. That had been a smart idea.

Road Crusher leaned over toward my ear and whispered with beer breath, "You have a real keeper here."

I felt myself go slightly faint. This elderly fellow had the mistaken idea that Cactus Ronnie and I were together like a couple, instead of me being here to experience a racetrack for the first time. I stole a glance at Ronnie as if that would tell me if he truly was a keeper.

Even as he stood talking to an old man, just shooting the breeze, he maintained a straight posture as though deeply rooted and confident in himself.

My heart pounded in my ears, clouding my hearing. I swallowed a lump in my throat, struggling to believe I was here at a racetrack in Tucson with a popular racer. This all seemed surreal.

Road Cruncher continued to tell me about who I was with. "Cactus Ronnie is the nicest guy in the world, and he deserves to find himself a nice woman." He looked into my eyes with an earnest intensity that made me jittery and extremely itchy.

This man acted like an old-fashioned mom trying to tie a knot with an available bachelor. I guess I was the bachelorette. Whatever. I needed to say something now to stop him.

"It's… not like… that," I stammered.

"You came here to see him, did you not?"

Prickles of discomfort shot through me as I glanced at Ronnie, who had pinkened maybe a shade or two underneath his tan cowboy hat. At least we shared our embarrassment.

"Actually, I just met him—like literally on the plane yesterday afternoon. We're just getting to know each other."

"Seriously?"

"Seriously."

Road Crusher laughed.

Feeling encouraged by the lighthearted nature of this gentleman and suspecting he wanted to banter, I added, "I have no idea what I've gotten myself into. But I have to say, it's good to hear he's a good guy. A girl can never be too careful."

To that, the old man smiled, revealing coffee-stained teeth. "Cactus Ronnie is a great guy. We all love him around here. That kid is going places. He's as determined and as committed as they come."

My eyes grew wide as I tried to subtly step away from this guy. Road Cruncher wasn't stopping the sales job on his buddy. Ronnie didn't look like he needed any help with the girls, but his friend apparently wanted to see him in a relationship and thought, for some reason, I was a good option.

"Crusher telling you lies?" Cactus Ronnie stepped up into our conversation.

My hairline dotted with sweat. I felt like I was about to climb out of my skin with him so near. I could smell his masculinity with a hint of gasoline, or maybe it was the addictive nitro.

Having Ronnie's and my nonexistent relationship as the center of attention, and having him stand so close, made my head swirl.

Road Crusher stood straighter. "Nope. Secrets about you." He nodded as he answered his friend, then took a swig of his beer from a plastic cup as if challenging him.

A smile crossed Ronnie's face, reaching his eyes. He had a natural charm about him. I could stare at that smile for a long time. He was carefree, relaxed, and yet somehow very focused.

"I hope it's all good then." Ronnie rested his arm around my shoulders, causing my whole body to tingle.

"So?" I raised my eyebrows toward Road Crusher, trying to keep my fast breathing from being noticed. "Cactus Ronnie here claims he's not a womanizer. Is that possibly true?"

Road Crusher looked at Cactus Ronnie and studied

him. "Come to think of it, it might be." He looked around and called out, "Phil?"

A middle-aged man with little hair and a tool in his hand stood up from whatever he was doing to the front end of the dragster next to us.

The man peered our way through the grease and sweat on his face.

"Have you seen Cactus Ronnie hanging with girls?"

Dragsters roared in the background as the crowd cheered. The man, waiting for the noise to die down, scratched the back of his head with the wrench. That made his white hair go in every direction.

"Never," he yelled back. "Why?"

"This little misses here is checking to see if Cactus Ronnie is giving her lines."

Ronnie shifted his weight as he glared back and forth between his friends.

I was pretty sure mine was not pink but red. I had a hard time keeping my head up as the wrench man chuckled.

"Good for her. Don't blame her. She could end up with the likes of me." He bent over his car again, quickly finished his work. He ambled over, pushing Cactus Ronnie aside. When inches from me, he whispered, "Cactus Ronnie is as good as it comes."

I forced a fake smile. This whole situation was getting out-of-control. "Thanks for letting me know."

He looked straight into my eyes. "I mean it. You're the first girl I've ever seen him with on the racing grounds. I don't think I've even seen him glance at any of the groupies that hang around here. Not even one lingering eye."

Wrench Man glanced at Cactus Ronnie and pressed his lips together. "His mind is always in the game. He's a true racer. No time for distractions." He waved to a group of men passing by, dressed in racing gear. "How's the track out there?"

The men stopped to tell Wrench Man about rods being kicked out of something.

Wrench Man and Cactus Ronnie shook their heads. "He's out for the weekend," Cactus Ronnie said. "That was one expensive mishap there."

Suddenly the crowd in the background erupted in a roar combined with stamping feet on the high risers.

The announcer yelled in the microphone, "Vincent 'Hammerhead' Krabull is going to the finals. He'll go head-to-head with Cactus Ronnie. Hammerhead ran a thousandth quicker than Ronnie. That means Vincent gets lane choice in the final round."

Road Cruncher leaned over to Ronnie and slapped him on the shoulder. "You'll get him."

Ronnie's lips had become thin, firm, pressed together. "It's not about him. It's about me and the car and how we're getting along. I have a jealous mistress. If I think even for a second about something else than her, she lets me know just how upset she is."

Wrench Man patted his stomach. "Our cars are certainly our mistresses."

The men nodded. Wrench Man turned to me again. "Dragsters take all our focus."

I nodded like I understood but didn't. There were certainly worse things for men to be obsessed about.

"He invited you here?" Wrench Man asked me.

I darted a glance at Ronnie. He gave me a quick nod like he heard the question and was okay with my answering the truth. If I wasn't mistaken, the pink color in his face had gotten deeper.

"Yes, sir."

"Then you must be something special."

I didn't know about that. Just lucky enough to win the lottery invite from Ronnie.

"You're different from the girls around here, that's for sure."

I shifted on my feet. "How so?" The sun was sinking, but not fast enough to hide the nervous twitch of my lips.

The man rubbed his hands together with a light-colored rag that quickly grew black.

"More innocent. More sweet. You seem to have a good sense of yourself. Some of the broads around here seem to be wandering aimlessly through life. I don't get that about you."

My throat tightened. He didn't think I was aimless? That made one of us.

Ronnie stepped up to us and grabbed my hand into his rough but gentle hand.

"Come on, jump on the four-wheeler. I'll show you the track. We have a little bit of time before we get cued. Let's take you on a spin through the racetrack."

The older men nodded at me. Confused, I stumbled after Ronnie. He squeezed my hand, sending a shiver up my arm. Even though I told Austin I would be seeing other boys, I flinched at holding another guy's hand. It only took a few moments, though, to let my hand relax into the touch.

As he guided us around a trailer where a couple of four-wheelers sat, Ronnie smiled at me. "How are you doing? This has got to be a bit much."

I looked coyly up at him, feeling an incredible wave of shyness, and nodded. He was right about that. It was a bit much. More than he knew. I'd never been good at juggling guys like some girls. I was a one guy sort of girl.

"What do you think?"

Besides the fact that Ronnie was gorgeous and my heart wouldn't stop pounding, I wasn't sure what to say. "About what?"

He paused for a brief moment. "Good question. What do you think about the racetrack?"

I shrugged. There was so much—noise, lights, people, dirt, and cacti—it was hard to even take it all in, let alone know what to make of it all.

"It's loud."

He smiled. "You'll get used to that. This stuff is just silly, but I like it."

"I can tell," I said.

He laughed. The dimple on his right cheek flashed when he laughed, carefree like that.

I hadn't seen Austin smile like that... maybe ever. Cactus Ronnie was a lot more easygoing. Seemed to be able to enjoy the moment more and hadn't mentioned his mom once yet. That was nice.

"I'll show you around if you're okay riding the four-wheeler with me." He gestured to a royal-blue hooded four-wheeler that looked ready to rumble.

My chest tightened as I thought about riding on the

back of a four-wheeler with a cowboy-racer-stranger. If my mom ever learned about this, she'd freak.

"Okay," I said weakly.

Ronnie hopped on the four-wheeler and waited for me to climb on behind him. When I hesitated, he gave me another smile, his trademark, springing another sighting of that dimple. There were a lot of people at this racetrack, maybe hundreds. It had to be safe for me to take a ride with him around this event, right?

As if reading my mind, he smiled at me, "I promise I won't hurt you."

I let out some air. Well, he had been at least able to read my mind. He held out his hand, palm up. "Here, let me help you."

I took his strong hand into mine, feeling the strength and the assurance of his grip. His firm touch caused my heart to pick up speed as though I'd gone racing down the track.

I managed to make it onto the four-wheeler, beads of sweat tracing my hairline and forming under my arms.

I took a quick inhale… nervous to be so close to him. I didn't dare take in a full lung of air. I was behind him, managing to not touch him, keeping a respectable distance apart—well, at least as much as could be managed on a four-wheeler.

He reached up with his right hand and pressed his cowboy hat firmly on his head before leaning in to me, his back bumping into my shoulder, causing sparks to shoot through me.

"You can hold onto me if you want. I want to make sure you're safe," he said.

I slid my camera strap around my neck until the camera hung down my back. Ronnie started the engine and let it roar before taking off at a slow speed. The engine happily puttered.

The wind tickled through my hair as we traveled by rows of other dragsters, large, expensive trailers that loomed in the darkening night, people hanging out on fold-out chairs drinking beer. The wind cooled my flushing face. Ronnie was a hottie, kind, and had dropped me into a foreign world as different from Idaho as I could imagine.

For one, it wasn't cold, which was nice. There were no thundering Teton mountains in the distance, just small ones. But, mostly, I wasn't surrounded by the suffocating quiet of eastern Idaho. Instead, everything was in commotion: noisy, dusty, and full of electricity.

The parking lot hadn't been paved, so every vehicle that drove on it stirred up more dirt. Everyone seemed to be humming with the thrill of seeing what a race car could do. The constant screams in the background amped up the thrill.

The four-wheeler suddenly slowed to a stop for an aimless pedestrian. The momentum thrust me into Ronnie's back, banging my cheek. I rubbed my face and hoped it wouldn't bruise.

"Sorry." Ronnie patted my leg. "Hold onto my waist, so that doesn't happen again."

My chest pounded. He wanted me to touch him. I took my hands off my face to grab onto the sides of his T-shirt with both hands. He took off again with a jolt.

I quickly wrapped my arms around his firm body. His

stomach was hard. Tight. Sexy. Warmth flooded me. My heart picked up speed again.

Ronnie turned his head. "Sorry about that. I'm not used to having a passenger."

I barely heard him as the wind whipped our faces and carried away his words. We said nothing more for a few minutes until he jerked to a halt to greet one of his associates.

And that was what we did. We stopped every couple of cars to say hi to someone, and they'd talk about how the weather affected the engines, who had great runs, who blew up an engine, and, of course, speed times. None of which made sense to me. It just sounded like them throwing around a lot of numbers.

I mostly said, "Hi." When asked what I thought of all this, I answered, "This is a lot."

It was. I felt like Alice in Wonderland falling down the rabbit hole, opening my eyes, and finding myself in a completely different world.

My comment about it being a lot earned a laugh every time.

Most of his friends looked back and forth between us while I flushed. Ronnie simply sat on the four-wheeler with his hands shoved partly into his pockets.

"Cactus Ronnie is a good guy." I heard that comment more than once.

Every time, I'd give an attempt at a smile and glance over at Ronnie, who looked at me with a subtle twinkle in his eye. I never could hold his gaze and ended up studying the ground.

One man said, "Have you seen this guy race? He's a beauty to behold."

Ronnie took his turn, looking at the ground, but a smile danced on his face. He scooted closer to me. "She'll see soon. Don't get her hopes up too much."

"I don't think I've ever seen Cactus Ronnie with a girl before. Are we going to see you again?" another guy asked. He bent forward as though wanting in on the scoop.

I leaned back as though I could get away from the question. "And I thought my mom liked to play matchmaker." With a scan of the men's interested expressions, I added, "You men have taken it to a whole new level. This is our first day."

Smiles and laughs rippled through them. "Seriously? What were you thinking, Cactus Ronnie, bringing her here with us?"

He put up his hands and shrugged. "Who said I was thinking?"

That earned more laughs.

Ronnie signaled it was time for us to move along, so I snuggled in again. We had almost reached the end of the line of parked dragsters when a dark-haired middle-aged man ran up to Cactus Ronnie with a wild glint in his eyes.

Ronnie introduced me to the man whose name was Paul. He nodded at me and muttered a, "Hi," followed by, "Have you seen Catherine?" He was looking around like a scared cat spooked over a dog on its tail.

"No," Ronnie said.

"I'm in a mess." He had a beer in a plastic cup and gulped.

"You're always in a mess," Ronnie said.

"Tell me about it. Both Nancy and Catherine are at this event. I brought Nancy, but Nigel told me Catherine is here, too, and she's madder than an exploding piston."

"Why?" Ronnie put on his problem-solving face, which I was becoming used to.

"I'm dating both of them."

Ronnie shook his head. "You need to backpedal off the ladies, man."

"Tell me about it. I'm going to be skinned alive." He looked around him like a hunted animal. "Gotta go."

Cactus Ronnie laughed. "I'll keep an eye out."

Paul nodded and walked away, glancing around in constant surveillance.

Cactus Ronnie whispered down at me. "Catherine is his former wife. They often do the rounds. Too much drama if you ask me, but it's funny to watch."

He pulled my arms around him tighter, causing my heart to lurch into my throat. We continued to do some rounds but, soon after, we made it to the end of the parking lot. Ronnie drove the four-wheeler into a field away from the track. He picked up speed.

I circled my arms around his taut waist and couldn't help but press my head against him, sending bolts of excitement through me. It felt good to lay my head on his strong back. Maybe I imagined things, but it seemed like he leaned into my touch as a much as I did.

We tore down a path, my hair flying behind me and Ronnie gripping the four-wheeler. He finally stopped in the middle of the field, turned off the vehicle, and climbed off. He peered at his watch.

I remained on the four-wheeler, nerves fluttering. I wasn't sure what he was up to.

"We have a few minutes before I have to get in line. You okay if we talk?"

I nodded and studied him with my head inclined to one side. "You sure love this stuff, don't you?"

He shrugged. "It passes the time. It's what I want to do."

"What's the goal?" I asked. "You want to win the big race? The championship?"

He neared the four-wheeler, his gaze connecting with mine. "Could. We'll see on that. I just want to race. Be with these machines. Listen to them talk and see if I can make them go."

"You talk like the machines have souls."

He looked at me with a straight face. "They don't?"

I didn't know what to say to that.

He stared off into the distance for a few minutes before saying, "So, what do you want out of life?"

Good question. One I didn't have an answer to. "I'm still exploring."

"That's good," he said. "Don't settle."

"Like I said before, my mom wants me to go to college. Get a degree."

He shuffled his feet. "Nothing wrong with that."

I lowered my head, not wanting to tell him I had planned to do that with Austin, but he left, and I was here because he wanted me to move to Tucson. Before whatever was going on between Ronnie and me went much further, I should probably tell him about Austin. That idea made my stomach instantly feel ill.

"Is that what you want to do?" Ronnie asked, bringing me back to the conversation.

I shrugged. "It's all confusing. I haven't figured it out. I guess I'm jealous of those people who just know what they want."

"It's a choice," Ronnie said.

"What do you mean?"

"You have to choose. Are you going to follow your passion, or are you going to do what everyone else tells you?"

I stared at him. "I should probably tell you something."

He stood taller. "Okay, tell me about it."

"I've been dating this guy. We were going to go to college together. Work on preserving this beautiful world of ours."

I waited for Ronnie to say something, get mad, or do something, but instead, he stood there waiting for me to finish what I was going to say. My heart thudded in my chest as I worked to find the words. Ronnie's silence wasn't making this easier.

But that wasn't his job, I thought suddenly. I didn't need people always trying to make things easier for me. I mean, I relied on that. I even wanted it sometimes. But I had a sudden blinding insight that maybe it wasn't all that good for me.

So, Ronnie standing there, listening, letting me form my own thoughts without doing it for me—him just standing there, not trying to make things easier—was... kind of amazing.

Didn't make it any more effortless to form the thoughts, though.

Flushed and high on drag racing and being able to form my own thoughts, I frowned as I slowly tried to explain to Ronnie, and maybe myself, what exactly was going on between Austin and me.

"Well, he got offered a job in Tucson. That's why I'm here. He asked me to come and see if I wanted to get a job at the company he works at. I did the interview today."

The moon spilled dark shadows on the earth. "Is that what you want?" Ronnie asked again.

My entire body was hot. My hands were warm, my skin felt electric. I had never thought about that before. What did I want? That was so hard to know.

"I don't know."

I didn't look into his eyes as I thought about my reluctance about the situation since Austin first took me on the canoe. Did I want Tucson and a corporate job? What if all my doubt wasn't about me not wanting to change? What if it was about my intuition telling me it wasn't the right path? The knots I had assumed were permanently lodged in my stomach loosened their grip. That might be the truth.

I looked up at Ronnie. "I don't think so." I smiled. A real one this time. I really didn't think so. Why hadn't anyone asked me what I wanted before? "That question is such a good one. Thank you."

He nodded like it wasn't that big a deal.

I looked at the dark sky. Oh, yeah, I was telling him bout Austin. He was going to think I was a hussy. I hurriedly added, "We have agreed to date other people."

I waited for Ronnie's response as he watched me. A few seconds passed before he simply said, "Okay," and climbed back onto the four-wheeler. "I recommend following your passion. That way, you'll have no regrets."

"What if I don't make it?" I wrapped my arms around him.

"Then, you tried. Nothing wrong with that."

He started the engine.

"Is that how you live your life?" I yelled over the engine noise.

"Always," he said. "I might not be the richest guy around, but I'm one of the happiest."

I wrapped my arms around him, confused at his response. He never said anything about my Austin story. He just told me to live my passion. I had certainly never met a guy like this before.

CHAPTER 8

*R*onnie grabbed my hand. "We're getting cued. Got to get my car in line."

I struggled to keep up with his accelerated pace as he beelined for basecamp. A group of older men stood in a coverall-clad circle already to spring into action.

"Ready to go?" one of them shouted.

"Let's go get 'em, Ronnie!" another called, pumping his fist in the air.

Overcome by excitement, I pumped mine back. Ronnie smiled down at me and fist-bumped my upraised hand.

I grinned bigger than I had in... forever.

I felt alive. Must be the nitro.

Ronnie slapped his hands together and rubbed them. "Game on."

The men shouted and hooted. I couldn't help but smile as I looked around, not sure what I was supposed to do now or where I'd go once he climbed into the car. Clearly, these cars were one-person only. I needed to make sure to stay out of the way of the great racer.

We hurried up to a long deep-blue race car with a longer nose than Road Crusher's.

"This is my dragster," Ronnie said with a proud smile.

I looked it over. It was shaped like a long, rectangular coffin, but thinner and longer, much longer, with a huge engine plopped in front of the seat.

Ronnie squeezed my hand. "Want to get in?"

"Don't you have to go now?"

"That was the call to get in line. We have some time. Everything is hurry up, and wait."

I looked at him, then over to the large tires surrounding the seat, and back to him. "How?"

He took my hand again and led me over. "Climb up onto the tire. You want to be careful not to step on the tinwork as you get in. That can damage easily."

I had to squeeze his hand tightly and lift my leg high to climb on the tire, which looked close to three feet at the top. He helped me up. I squealed with my heart racing.

"Avoid the tin work."

I raised my eyebrows. "How?"

"Step onto the bottom of the seat."

I did as instructed, standing there with a bit of a wobble. This was a lot harder than I thought it would be.

"Now put both hands on top of the frame rails."

"The what?"

He patted the frame where the doors should have been. I put my hands on it and squatted.

"Kick one leg over the axle housing, then the other, and drop yourself into the seat."

I huffed. He was still talking a foreign language. "The what?"

Ronnie pointed his finger at a long thing that went side to side inside the car right in front of the seat.

I sat all the way down and put one leg out then the next, hoping I was getting close to what he was instructing.

"Like that?" I asked.

He gave a short nod. "Good enough."

There was absolutely no wiggle-room in the seat. Putting my hands on the steering wheel, I looked up like I was going to drive, but I couldn't see anything in front of me. A massive engine totally blocked my view. I couldn't even see the front of the race car. That was crazy. How could anyone drive fast if their vision was blocked?

"How do you see when there's a big engine in the way?"

Cactus Ronnie smiled. "Most of the time, you don't. You have to look at the lines to your left or your right."

No way. I couldn't imagine driving down the racetrack going the speeds the racers go without being able to see where I was headed. Just the thought made my breath catch. That was insane, yet Ronnie did it all the time, and with a smile.

"You've got to be kidding me," I said. "You go how fast without seeing where are you going?"

"Well, a slow run would be above two hundred miles per hour."

I stared, mouth open. "How..." I cleared my throat. "How does anyone get down the track without killing themselves if they can't see?"

Ronnie laughed. "You're traveling fast. The car is eating up real estate quickly." He sighed. "How can I explain it?"

I butted in, "How do you know where you're going?"

He sighed. "By looking at the guardrail and the center-line. You can just tell where you're at."

That, I would have to think about—a lot.

"That sounds so scary."

Ronnie smiled. "You know, theoretically, there's nothing in front of you while going down the track. It's about trusting yourself, the car, and knowing what you are capable of. Sometimes, you just have to let go of control, Darlene. That's the only way to really experience the rush of life and fully embrace it."

Let go of control? Embrace life? I always hid. Maybe that was why I wasn't going anywhere. Maybe that was why I felt so stuck.

He clapped his hands together. "We need to get going. Would you be willing to steer the car as we line it up?"

My eyes grew large. "I'm not sure how to do that."

"Just keep the steering wheel straight. It's easy. I'll tell you how to make any adjustments." He looked into my eyes with such a twinkle I couldn't help but make my eyes twinkle back at him.

"Of course."

I was about to drive a race car.

Ronnie patted me on the head and turned to shoot orders to the guys around him. "We need to line up." He climbed back onto his four-wheeler, pulling it in front of his car.

Working in a fluid motion, as though involved in a well-choreographed performance, he hooked a towing rope to the front of the race car and attached that to the four-wheeler.

The guys gathered behind the car. Ronnie hopped onto

the four-wheeler, all business now, the tension thick. My palms became clammy on the steering wheel. He wanted me to pilot this car, and I couldn't even see beyond the engine. He was trusting me to keep his car safe before his big race. That might not be smart on his part.

I sat up straighter, hoping to see what I could around the engine. Ronnie had talked about trust. That probably didn't involve getting his race car through the pit area.

On cue from Ronnie, the men who had gathered in behind started pushing the car. One of them hurried to my side and grabbed hold of the steering wheel, turning it with force to make the turn out of the campsite.

"This is such a long vehicle you don't want to turn when you think you normally would. You have to go farther out to make room for the nose."

That made sense.

I blinked, not daring to take my eyes off of Ronnie, who, fortunately, I could see above the engine.

The race car picked up speed as Ronnie turned back and shouted more orders. "Make a tighter right corner."

This time I took the reins, jaw clamped down tight and yanked the wheel farther to the right. No flinching, no doubt, I simply did what needed to be done to be part of the team.

After rounding the corner with no hiccups, Ronnie signaled me with a thumbs up.

A smile burst across my face, and I wasn't going to hide it. I was doing it. I was steering a dragster without the ability to see in front of me. I was heading blindly toward the racetrack without stewing, hemming, and hawing.

I continued steering, aware of a crowd of onlookers,

most likely wishing they were steering the dragster instead of me. I didn't let that distract me from following the cues Ronnie issued.

As the journey went on, I slipped into the rhythm and no longer had a crew member lean over to correct my steering.

I was doing this.

Once out of the camp, the rope that tugged the car straightened, and people cleared a path out of our way, turning to see our journey toward the racetrack.

"Go, Cactus Ronnie!" screamed a rather beautiful girl, probably closer to Ronnie's age than I.

Ronnie waved to her.

The man who helped me steer earlier continued to walk beside the car. "You're a natural," he told me. "We might have another race car driver on our hands. You're driving her like a pro."

Under different circumstances, I might have taken a moment to wonder why men always called their cars "her," but I let it go. All my focus stayed on keeping the car straight, following Ronnie.

The task turned out to be easier than I thought. Other racers rolled their race cars to the lanes along with us.

Ronnie stopped the four-wheeler. A crew member pulled on a handle in the car, preventing the race car from hitting the four-wheeler. I stayed in the car as people strolled by us.

A lot of people stopped to stare at me with almost envious looks. One lady ran up and asked, "How did you get to sit in the race car?"

"Um," I said, "I know the owner."

"You're so lucky!"

I guess, to many people, I was. I settled back into the uncomfortable seat.

"I always wanted to know what it was like to sit in one of those," a passing woman commented.

I shifted in my seat and called back, "Uncomfortable!"

Ronnie parked the four-wheeler behind the race car and came over to join me.

The lady called out to him. "Good luck out there!"

He waved, clearly not giving the woman much thought, and turned to me. "You okay?"

I gave him two thumbs up and a grin.

A Hawaiian shirt approached. He wore a whistle on a lanyard tied around his neck. "Time to line up."

Ronnie's jaw tightened as a serious expression flickered through his face. "You need to climb out. I'm getting cued that it's close to my turn."

I looked at the big tires couching me into the seat, ready to do as requested. "How?"

Ronnie looked back at me. "Oh, yeah. I guess you need help. Put your arms up on the frame and hoist yourself up. Remember to be careful where you step."

He leaned over and helped me as I pulled up until my underarms rested on the frame and hauled myself out of the seat. The metal bit back.

"Ouch!" I yelped as he helped me to my feet. I found myself standing on the leather seat. "What do I do now?"

Ronnie held out his hand. "Climb up on the big tire."

He had to be kidding.

He grabbed my hand and pulled me firmly onto the tire. I wobbled on top of it until Ronnie grabbed my torso and hugged me to him as he swung me to the ground.

"Oh-h!" I laughed, finding my feet.

"You good?" Ronnie checked on me again.

"I am."

I noticed how his eyes sparkled as he led me to the four-wheeler and helped me climb on. He told me I'd done a great job.

A few minutes later, out of nowhere, one of the younger-looking men on the team, though with thick silver hair, ran toward me. His kind hazel eyes caught my gaze as he hopped on the four-wheeler, causing it to dip under his weight. He sat a respectful distance in front of me, started the vehicle, and inched it forward until a metal pad on the front bumped against the race car and pushed it.

I seized the back metal bar, gripping tight, not sure of what I had just gotten myself into. I jumped as the race car engine started. Its thundering noise pierced my ears, hurting them. I let go of the metal bar to cover my ears. The four-wheeler lurched forward again, and the front metal pad banged against the race car, pushing the long rectangular car forward into the night. Cactus Ronnie steered to the right, lining up to the racetrack.

Another loud, crackling car rolled up to our left, preparing for the duel.

My four-wheeler driver nudged the car to a point far behind the starting line of the track. Once finished, he sped to the outside of the guardrail, with me behind him, trying to maintain my balance and still hold my ears.

After he climbed off, he dug into his pocket and pulled

out a package of earplugs, which he handed to me. Signaling an "okay" gesture with his forefinger and thumb, he hurried off to stand on the racetrack directly in front of Cactus Ronnie's dragster.

Ronnie hurried over to the four-wheeler to grab his fire suit out of a duffle bag, pulled out a pair of black pants, which he tugged on over his jeans. That had to be hot in this toasty weather.

"I'm going up against one of the best drivers in this league," he shouted to me in an unshakeable, matter-of-fact way.

He sure kept cool under pressure. As he assembled himself, other older men gathered around him and me, talking shop and helping him dress.

I tried to stay out of the way.

"Bill," Ronnie said to the man who'd driven me on the four-wheeler. "This is Darlene. She's with us tonight."

Bill smiled. "Good for you. You're in for an adventure hanging out with this fellow, aren't you?"

I didn't know what to say, but it turned out I didn't need to say anything.

Ronnie took control. "Can she ride with you on the four-wheeler after my run?"

They quickly worked out what to do with me. I was assigned to stay on the four-wheeler, which was next to the race car, while Cactus Ronnie raced. The knot that I hadn't been paying too much attention to in my stomach loosened. I at least knew what my job was through this whole thing—stay on the four-wheeler.

Ronnie nodded at me. "Bill will be with you soon."

I followed my orders and sat watching as Ronnie and

his team ran through a checking system. We were quickly becoming the next in line. An ample overhead light blared onto a shining black straight racetrack.

Men with official-looking shirts and carrying radios patrolled the lanes where we parked. A booth nested high in the far corner to the side of the track housed the commentator.

One of Ronnie's guys approached and gestured for me to follow him. "Come look."

He strode to the corner of the racetrack where a gate separated us from the thousands of spectators. "This is where you'll come with Bill. Look at all those people who have paid to watch Ronnie do his thing. It's amazing, isn't it?"

I stared at the packed stands. It was incredible, and I was there witnessing it all because I decided to dodge a party.

The guy nudged me. "We better get back."

As we hustled back, my heart thudded. I returned to find Ronnie completely masked, standing by the race car. He held out his hand to me, and I took it. He squeezed my fingers.

"Be safe," I heard myself saying over the roar of the cars. Way too much emotion choked my throat.

He squeezed my fingers again.

A signal must have come because suddenly, Cactus Ronnie had slipped into the car. I couldn't believe how quickly he made it in.

Men assisted him with the safety harness, black gloves, a helmet, and goggles.

A flood of nerves coursed through me. I was about to

witness my first live race, and with Cactus Ronnie behind the wheel.

This was hardcore. Much more dangerous than a canoe ride down the Snake River in the dark, no matter how threatening I thought it was at the time.

Cactus Ronnie gave a thumbs-up signal, setting Bill off to hustle to the side of the race car. He squirted something into the engine, and a loud noise erupted from the machine. He fiddled with the engine, and the dragster shook alive, like a gigantic monster waking.

It shook hard as it idled. The movement was violent, and large yellowish-white flames jetted out of the car's side pipes, letting everyone know to stay away.

A lady with red hair flowing down her back and long purple fingernails hurried over with a large camera. She snapped pictures of the rattling flames spewing forth from the machine.

Her hair spilled in front of her shoulders as she aimed the camera at the crackling beast. The track lighting cast a glow on the dragster.

Cactus Ronnie hunkered down behind the steering wheel, now a mystery man with a black helmet, mask, and goggles hiding his identity, which the photographer captured from many different angles.

What did she see? I swung my camera case back to my front and pulled out the camera, wanting to see what she saw.

She did a furious round of picture taking before leaving to capture another side of the race car.

I remained silent as I hung back but couldn't help stepping up and holding my camera to my eye to help imagine what she saw. I smiled. From that angle, she found a way to contrast the blue of the car with the dark of the night and the flames of the rocking machine.

Also, seeing Ronnie's intense eyes through his goggles looked super dope. I wanted that photo, too, maybe just for myself.

I snapped a round of pictures to see if I could find the groove of the professional's technique.

The photographer leaned in and squatted down by the large tires. I imitated her and noticed how more angles emerged in the camera lens, revealing a completely different nature of the dragster. She used composition and lighting in more ways than just capturing the image.

When she moved on to the next car, I looked back to see Cactus Ronnie's focus zeroed-in on what was ahead of him. He did not pay attention to the photographer, me, his friends.... nothing but the track in front of him. That, I could learn from. The man didn't allow himself to be side-tracked. No doubt lay in those eyes. Only a ferocious determination as his mind fastened onto the track and the upcoming round.

My fingers vibrated. I flicked a glance around me. Everyone watched Ronnie. I slipped the camera up again without looking away from him. I smiled as I freeze-framed that moment. Loud monster machines split ahead of us and roared, tearing at my eardrums.

After capturing the dramatic focus of this racer with my camera, I dug from my pocket the earplugs Bill had provided and put them in to escape the fierce roar.

When I looked up again, Bill signaled it was time to go.

I hustled back to the four-wheeler, heart-pumping, and

looked back at the race car. Ronnie was actually going to do this. He was going to tear down the track going better than two hundred miles an hour.

Fear drove through me faster than the race cars, and my throat tightened.

I blinked as I looked over at Ronnie. From this angle, I could see nothing about him behind the mask and the fire suit. I did nothing to catch his attention, not wanting to distract him.

He could crash. He could...

Fire roared out of his car.

The dragster gave a violent shudder.

The ground vibrated from the force, feeling like an earthquake tremor.

My entire body trembled. Sweat coated my skin. Dragsters caused a much larger inferno than I had ever imagined, and Ronnie sat in the center of it and was about to drive straight into the heart of the explosion.

Trembling, I put my camera into its case, zipped it up, and flipped it onto my back again, preparing for my own ride. My fingers curled tightly around the back bar of the four-wheeler.

Blackness hovered over the track. The dark bumped up against the bright white lights pouring onto the driving lanes below. The cheers from the stands increased in volume as the anticipation climaxed for the big showdown.

Flags waved, and noise from the dragsters tore at eardrums as both cars shook the ground.

Professional photographers, and people carrying TV cameras, captured the scene from mere feet away from those beasts. They were so close they could surely feel the beast's breath.

As I watched the photographers and TV people work, all I could think about was how I wanted to risk the charging bull, too. I could create some stunning pictures.

The yearning swelled in my chest so intensely I could taste my longing. I took out my camera again and, through the lens, searched for the right angle, spot, and frame. A smile slipped across my lips.

This I loved. This, snapping pictures of power, smoke, and red-hot flames, all mixed with the drama of excitement and fear. It boiled together to produce a peak of anticipation. I wanted more of this. This was an amazing place to capture something rare, unique, and scary.

The track, smelling of hot asphalt and smoke, created a haunting mood. I itched to capture it with my camera by moving up closer, but everything seemed so official, and I certainly didn't want to stumble into a place where I didn't belong. I stayed on the four-wheeler as instructed.

Was Cactus Ronnie thinking about me behind the wheel, looking for where I was? Or was his focus completely on the task in front of him? I wouldn't want him to crash because he wasn't paying attention. But he was a professional. I was sure he had it down.

Traffic-like lights on a tall gadget in front of the race cars flickered. The noise level of the crowd swelled. This was it.

My stomach seized. What if Cactus Ronnie got hurt? What if he ran into the two-foot cement wall I sat behind? Could the car flip and hit me?

The announcer came over the intercom. "We have

Cactus Ronnie in the right lane. He's an all-time local favorite and a class champion in multiple events. He just loves to speed down the lane. Keep an eye on him, folks. I'm sure he'll not disappoint."

His car shook with a fierceness as his tires spun. The car tore ahead for about a hundred fifty feet. Smoke rose, and burning rubber filled the muggy air. As the long silhouette of the car started backing up, Bill suddenly jumped ahead of it on the track, frantically giving hand signals. Long flames shot out of the engine. The noise was deafening. Cactus Ronnie's car stopped, then slowly inched forward as Bill's hand guided the car to the starting line.

"And we have the new driver, Vincent 'Hammerhead' Kraball, who just beat Ronnie in the semi-final from Salt Lake City, Utah. We need to keep an eye on him, folks."

The opponent's car burst ahead on the asphalt, taking its turn, filling the track with smoke. He had someone in front of him signaling like Bill had just done for Ronnie. The red dragster settled in its lane with the staccato roar of its engine almost as loud as Cactus Ronnie's car.

Bill walked off to the side and behind Ronnie's car as the stoplight gadget in the middle of the lanes flashed yellow. A moment later, it flashed green.

Both cars accelerated ahead with a ground-shaking, ear-pounding roar, leaving tire smoke trailing behind. It was impossible to see anything but the cars disappearing into the darkness. The audience members in the stadium stomped their feet.

The announcer screamed over the intercom. "He did it! Cactus Ronnie just had an amazing run. He ran 5.68 at 263 mph. This ensures he'll go to the finals."

The crowd erupted.

I steepled my hands together. He made it. He did it. He was safe.

"I told you, folks! He won't disappoint," added the announcer.

As I was trying to recover my heartbeat to a normal pace, and pulled out my earplugs, Bill ran up to the four-wheeler with the largest smile. He slapped his hands together. Shaking his head, he climbed on the four-wheeler. "That was amazing."

Before I knew it, I clung to his waist as we tore down a long flat stretch of pavement in front of a roaring, waving crowd. Not expecting to be part of the show, I shook off my embarrassment of being watched by so many people and waved back.

The four-wheeler arrived at the end of the dark and shadowy racetrack. Bill climbed off and looked at me. "I want to tell you, because you may not know this, but Cactus Ronnie is an absolutely amazing person. Besides being a great driver, he's the kindest guy I know. He's the type of guy who would give you the shirt off his back without thinking twice."

* * *

AFTER GOING through the whole routine again, Cactus Ronnie and Bill won the final round. The announcer bid his farewells until the next race, and the stadium rapidly emptied of its very enthusiastic crowd. Some of the spectators had migrated over to the race cars, talking and grinning as they surveyed the machines with approving nods.

A few of the brave gawkers asked a question or two about the car, parts, or the actual racing.

Bill took me back to Ronnie, who greeted me with a large smile. "Did you like it?"

"It was intense," I said.

He chuckled and pulled me to him, hooking my hand around his forearm, which sent warmth through my palm and beyond. Onlookers had gathered, wanting to ask questions. He patiently answered each person like a perfect gentleman. Periodically, he'd glance at my hand like he was making sure we were still connected.

Despite all the buzz around me, the endless talk of cars and engines caused my mind to wander. What was I getting myself into? But when Ronnie squeezed my hand, his comforting touch drew my attention back to him.

As he continued the conversations, I received a couple of jealous looks from gawking female fans, and I returned those with smiles.

Once, when one of the onlookers dove into long details about dragster history, Ronnie mouthed a thanks to me. I couldn't help but smile shyly back at him, too.

After the last admirer had left, he hooked his arm around my neck. "I promised you a fire-up. We need to do that."

My stomach squeezed into a knot. "That's okay," I said. "It's getting late."

He pulled me closer to him until my face pressed into his black T-shirt. "A promise is a promise."

By this time, the track was almost empty, with only racers and their crews messing around with their cars. Most were loading up everything into trailers.

Ronnie seized my hand and walked me to the camp where his race car still sat.

Paul passed by us. He was alone, shaking his head. "Don't ever date two of them at once, Ronnie. Just don't do it. It's not worth it, man."

Ronnie laughed. "Okay. I won't." He squeezed my hand as we headed away from his dejected friend.

A tall, slender guy, around my age, went by.

"Andy," Ronnie called out, "have you seen Bill?"

Andy stopped, took a breath, and looked around the mostly empty staging area. "I think he was over there finishing up with Earl."

Ronnie squeezed my hand. "Wait here. I'll be right back."

No more than six minutes later, the silhouettes of both men headed toward me. I had grown tired of standing and had climbed on the four-wheeler.

As I yawned, the side door snapped open. "Time."

I gulped, looked at him, and passed him toward patient Bill. As I maneuvered off of the vehicle, I asked, "What's a fire-up?"

Ronnie grinned. "Where you start the car and see how it runs."

I remembered now how he had explained it on the plane, but I hadn't realized his offer was serious at the time. I hurriedly placed my camera on the four-wheeler and moseyed over to the two men, who fiddled with the race car under the track lighting.

Bill smiled at me as he handed me a fire jacket to put on. I slipped into the black jacket, feeling immediately hotter.

Cactus Ronnie came up to my right side. "Now it's time to climb into the car."

He took my hand as I scrambled on top of the tire.

"Watch the tinwork," I was instructed again.

Eventually, I sat in the car, squished and unable to move, with a seatbelt fastened.

Some late stragglers passing by saw what we were doing and stopped to ogle. By this point, Cactus Ronnie put his hand on my shoulder, which stopped the continuous tightening of my stomach. The darkness of the evening crowded around us.

Fortunately, Ronnie still stood beside me. His dark features and wavy black hair were hard not to stare at. My throat constricted as I waited for whatever was going to happen.

Cactus Ronnie stood in front of me to my right. "We need to get the helmet on."

He handed me a heavy helmet that I tugged onto my head.

"Gloves and goggles, too." Ronnie held out some for me.

I grabbed them and tried to put them on.

Ronnie reached in. "Let me tighten them for you. I know it is tricky to figure out."

I held my arms out like a helpless baby, and he fastened up the gloves and placed the goggles over my eyes.

He leaned into the cockpit. "When I give you the thumbs-up signal, I want you to flip that silver switch there on your left, okay?" He handed me a clean rag. "Use this to cover your mouth and nose. And, when I give the 'cut' signal, push the handle right there." He pointed.

With the helmet on, I felt like I was deep-sea diving on

a different planet, so I nodded. My breath came out harsh and ragged, betraying the building panic that rose in my chest. My rapid breathing steamed up the helmet's visor.

I closed my eyes, trying not to think about how small space I was pinned in. Many racers were much bigger than I not only sat in these seats but drove, flying two hundred miles per hour down the track, not even being able to see what was in front of them.

My focus remained completely on Ronnie. If he could do this going two hundred miles an hour, I could do this just sitting in the stationary dragster.

My goggles also fogged up from my heavy breathing. I blinked from the gas itching my eyes. My gaze stayed on Ronnie.

Bill squirted the engine with the squirt bottle. The engine roared from the fluid. I tried to blink the sweat out of my eyes as I gripped the steering wheel, anxious, grabbed the cloth to wipe my eyes after this was over.

Cactus Ronnie gave the signal, an animated thumbs up. My heart lurched. Closing my eyes, I flipped the switch on the dashboard.

The car erupted into an earthquake shake, exploding to life. It shook like an Indian rattle determined to bring rain. My heart lurched nearly out of my chest as I tried to hold onto the steering wheel while on the most acute roller coaster ride of my life.

After a long rattle, I peeked up to Ronnie to see him doing something with the engine. Before I could think about it, the dragster took on an angrier shake, making my brain feel like it might scramble.

Large flames erupted from the ends of the pipes, increasing the temperature to what hell must feel like. Sweat poured from everywhere on my body. Tears and mascara streamed down my face as fumes sprayed across my mask. The most violent fear gripped me tightly, refusing to let go.

The noise catapulted to a decibel level, louder than anything I'd ever heard before. My eyes burned. I could hardly make out the shaking world in front of me.

As my stomach whirled, I peered through the goggles of the black mask and stared out at the men, and a growing crowd. The car bit with anger, jolting, ready to tear down the road.

I closed my eyes to lessen the sting, then opened them again to see Ronnie give the "cut" signal. Fingers trembling, I pulled the handle he had pointed out to me earlier. The engine sped up in a low hum and stopped.

In the midst of this raucous experience, the night fell into a dead silence. The crowd erupted in applause as my heart trotted toward normal speed. I had survived. I pulled off the gloves, and the helmet, and a huge unexpected smile lit my face.

"Wow!" My entire body shook.

Time to exit the car. I struggled to figure out how to extract myself, and at last, raised my hands.

Ronnie was soon by my side, pulling me out like my hero. I made it into his arms but, instead of enjoying the moment, I gave in to the hard trembling caused by all the power that had just channeled through me. That bronco ride had been extraordinary.

When I had calmed down a bit later, I walked over to

the four-wheeler to retrieve my camera and watch the aftermath.

As most of the onlookers left and his crew started to pack up, Ronnie came up to me. "You appear to be my good luck charm." His face drew close to mine.

There was something so sexy in the way he had just claimed me. He put his arms around my torso and pulled me to him like he knew exactly what he wanted... me. I felt the tug to kiss him. His lips neared mine.

"Do you mind if I kiss you?" he whispered.

"No," I whispered back, my voice almost failing me as the tension between us built.

Ronnie firmly leaned in until his lips met mine. Determination seeped through him and zapped me. I kissed back as he reached around to place his hand in my hair and pull me closer toward him. As he pressed us together, an intense longing rushed through me. My head swam.

I had never kissed anyone like that before, and I definitely wanted more. I wanted more of *all* of this. Not the racing—I really didn't see myself as a race car driver in the future. But the excitement, the extreme focus, the intensity, being surrounded by people doing exactly what they loved... independence.

I felt free.

CHAPTER 9

A proud smile merged onto Ronnie's face when he pulled away. "We did good." He hooked his arm around me, pulling me into his toned body again.

I leaned into his touch, absorbing his happiness. "That we did."

He nodded. "You were a great help. You steered the car into the lineup like a pro."

I wasn't sure about all that, but at least he was happy with my involvement. "I was surprised at how snug the seats are. It's like they want to hold you in tight."

"Safety first." His fingers started to stroke my back in little gentle movements, which shot a tingle through my skin. His dimple creased. "I mean it about taking the car out. It normally takes a person a little bit to catch on that the car needs to be steered differently, but you were shown once," he snapped his fingers, "and you got it. Maybe you have a racer inside of you yet."

I rolled my eyes, not telling him his friend had said that, too. I doubted I'd ever be a racer, but a photographer... A shiver of hope rose in me with that idea. I'd always considered it as just a dream. But Ronnie was living his dream.

He broke into my thoughts when he took his hand off my back. "I need to finish up the trailer and race car. It might take a while. Would you mind waiting? I'll take you to the hotel, or for food, or whatever you want after we finish."

His gaze searched mine.

I looked away. Ronnie was a stranger. The smart thing to do would be to call a taxi. I should go home. I should go to bed and forget all of this happened.

"You'll be safe, promise." His expression looked so sincere. And, almost everyone had told me—unprompted —what a good guy he was.

I lowered my gaze. What would it hurt to stay out a little longer? Just for one more night? I had already snuck out. A few more hours wouldn't matter.

I'd probably never see him again. This was my one chance to just be in this world and with him. To take a risk.

"I'll wait," I whispered.

He pulled me into another kiss. A quick one. "I'll hurry. Promise."

"What can I do to help?"

Ronnie patted my shoulder, sending another zing of excitement through me. "We have a smoothly run system, and I don't want you to get hurt."

He grabbed my hand. Our fingers intertwined like it was the most natural thing in the world. "Come on." Cactus Ronnie took off walking with quick, broad steps, making it hard to keep up with him. He pulled me around to the front end of a Chevy truck and opened the door. "Rest in here."

I climbed in, following to trust him and do what he said. Maybe I wasn't trusting him but, instead, trusting myself to know I could have really cool experiences if I listened to my intuition.

Ronnie climbed up on the running board and leaned over my lap, not touching me. I held my breath, not sure what he was doing.

He started the truck and flipped on the heater. "It's getting chilly." He climbed back down and stood between the door and me.

"Won't be long, promise." He winked and hurried away, trusting me to be fine. Just like he trusted I could steer his car and take care of myself when he was racing down the track. The man treated me like I could handle things. He didn't hover. He didn't doubt. He didn't pressure me to make a decision.

Thinking about it made my heart swell. There was something deeply attractive about his ability to see the real me, the person I was capable of being, and not questioning or trying to change me. I wondered if Ronnie was always like that. Was that part of why all these people thought he was a good guy? He just believed in people.

When I caught a glimpse of myself in the rearview mirror, I marveled again that I was here... at a racetrack in Tucson far away from the silence of nature in the Rocky Mountains and the bitter cold of Idaho. I had spent so long in isolation there it felt invigorating to be here with all these people... all these nice older guys fussing about race cars.

The crew moved in a dance, picking up cords and working on the race car in a flow that led to other tasks. Each person knew their part and had their timing down as they labored under the glow of the overhead yellow lights.

I watched for a while, but couldn't resist any longer and turned off the engine. Grabbing my camera, and slipping the truck key into my back pocket, I climbed out of the truck into the dark shadows several feet away from the men. I looked through my lens and hunted for the perfect shot.

It would come to me. If I let it speak to me. I had to give it time and not worry what anyone thought of me.

I held the camera steady, then as high as my height would allow, and angled it down to get a god's eye view. I peered over to the men and the car. Better. Cut the car and men in half. The picture needed to be filled with angles. Diagonals. I shuffled to my left. Even better.

I snapped. A flash emanated from the camera, catching the racers unaware. They looked at me. *Snap.* Shock registered on their faces. *Snap.*

Bill called out. "We have our own photographer."

More heads turned toward me.

"That'll be great," someone else called out. "I hope they turn out in the dark."

I didn't get distracted by their comments. *Snap.*

Bill put chords down and came over to me. I stopped taking pictures, preparing to be reprimanded.

"Can you make sure I get some copies? I'd love to blow them up for my garage. I always wanted a night shot of this."

A small smile crossed my face. "Sure."

"The crew will love them."

My stomach twisted. I had no idea if any of my pictures were any good. "I'm not sure if they'll turn out."

"They'll be great."

These racers sure seemed confident. I snapped more pictures of Ronnie and Bill, and the crew as they tucked everything into place. Once they were finished, I climbed into the passenger side of Ronnie's truck, clinging to my camera.

Thinking about photography, I leaned back in the passenger seat and rested my eyes until Ronnie climbed into the truck, ready to go.

I yawned.

A tiny hint of disappointment crossed his features. "Do you want me to take you back to the hotel, or would you possibly be up for joining the gang at a twenty-four-hour breakfast joint for a late-night bite of food?"

"I'll join you." I gave him a bashful smile.

That lit up his face. "It'll be late."

"That's okay," I said, not able to hold back a bigger smile.

Not much later, I found myself in one of those rundown all-night cafés couched in the middle of numerous racers and crew members all talking enthusiastically over one another. Nursing a hot tea, I listened to everyone's wild racing tales and managed to stifle most of my yawns. The stories continued, and I started to get itchy. I pulled out my camera and flipped through the pictures taken during the evening.

Ronnie noticed and broke away from glory-day tales. "Can I take a look?"

I handed him the camera.

"How do I go through them?"

I showed him the button to go back and forth.

He looked them over. "You are good."

I felt heat break out to race up the back of my neck. "Thanks."

"Every one of your pictures captures frozen moments."

I took the camera from him and flipped through them. They were. "Been experimenting with that," I muttered.

"I'd like to see your photos that show movement, too," Ronnie said.

I flipped through my pictures, not only from tonight, but all the pictures I had taken in the past few months. Every single photo I had taken froze the moment.

I took a sip of my tea. Why had I done that? What would catching movement instead of freezing things be like? What would I have to adjust in the camera to make that work?

I thought about that for a long time as the stories continued. I could see the deep passion when it was Ronnie's turn. He explained to them, down to the very last detail, how the driver thought before a race, and the actions he took to move best down the track. I loved the sparkle shining in his eyes as he spoke.

After I finished my tea, I grew very sleepy, and my head and eyelids kept dropping down. I slumped against my purse, and leaned my head back against the restaurant cushion. I closed my eyes.

Ronnie noticed eventually because when I blinked my eyes open, he said, "Looks like I'm getting the signal it's time to get the little lady home."

"Ah, I'm calling it a night, too," Bill said.

Everyone agreed, and each person threw a wad of cash on the table for the waitress.

Ronnie smiled at me. "Let's get you to your room."

I stumbled after him. The other fellows waved goodbye and congratulated Ronnie. He thanked them and said good night before opening the door to his truck.

I climbed in, and we drove a ways with the radio playing eighties music.

"Where to?" Ronnie asked.

I managed to look up the hotel name and relay the address. Before I knew it, he had pulled into the parking lot. He helped me out of the truck and insisted on walking me to my room. "I'd feel more comfortable seeing you safely inside."

I nodded, hoping he didn't want to come into my room or expect something more, but my worry was unfounded. We made it back to my room a little after two in the morning. We kissed another half a dozen times in the hotel hall, each passionate, each addictive. Then he turned to go.

"I'll call you," he said.

I nodded, sleepily gazing up at him. I hoped he would and that this wouldn't be a one-nighter. "Good night, Ronnie. Thank you for an amazing night."

"Good night, Dari." He winked at me.

His nickname for me made my lips turn up at the corners.

I waited to look at my phone until I was behind the hotel door and on my bed. I didn't want Austin, and all that was going on there, to bleed into my time with Ronnie.

To my surprise, I only found one text from Austin: *Hey,*

where are you? But there were phone calls, too. Two, to be exact. "Darlene, where are you?" came slurred words over the phone. "We can't find you, and we're worried. JT has gotten on his four-wheeler to look for you."

That didn't sound good, and I certainly didn't want the next step, which was for them to call the police. I quickly texted back: *I'm fine. In my hotel room.* I turned off my phone, feeling incredibly excited about the evening, and not able to think about anything but the thrill of fresh experiences, and the joy I felt when snapping photos. And, of course, Ronnie's spine-tingling kisses.

I didn't need to leave to catch the plane until tomorrow afternoon. Until then, I'd dream about the racetrack and Ronnie.

Four hours later, a little after six in the morning, a loud series of bangs sounded on my door. I had been sleeping, dreaming about a kiss from Ronnie, and anxious about what to do with Austin. Ronnie and Austin's faces had blurred together, tugging at me in my dreams.

In my PJs, I stumbled toward the door and peered through the peephole. I opened the door to a disheveled Austin as he stumbled into the room. "Where did you go?" he asked.

Walking past him, I walked back to sit on the edge of the bed. "You were ignoring me, and since I was finally out of Island Park and in the big city, I thought I'd go have some fun on my only night here." I tried to speak matter-of-factly, but tears rose up in my voice. "Austin, you completely shut me out. I didn't know anyone. At one time, you bumped me like I was in your way."

"I did?" He paled as he came over to sit next to me. "I'm

sorry, Dar." He took me into his arms and held me. I wanted to resist, but I couldn't. I curved into his chest. I tried to speak, but he hushed me. "I'm sorry, baby. I didn't want you to feel that way."

"You drank too much."

"I know." He buried his face on top of my head, breathing in my hair. "I care about you, and I missed you so much." His arms tightened around me. "I need you." His voice cracked.

Austin had never been like this before. Clearly, all the transitions had been tough on him, too. It must be hard to move to a new place, take on a new job, and deal with a soon-to-be stepdad/boss.

I squeezed his arm. "It's okay."

I tipped my head back for a kiss, pushing away the guilt I felt about kissing Ronnie a few hours earlier.

* * *

WE KISSED FOR A LONG WHILE, then Austin helped me pack and waited for me to get ready. He took me to breakfast, and after eating, we stayed in each other's arms, sitting in the booth, not daring to say much.

Me thinking of him, Ronnie, Tucson, and my possible new work at a place I had no interest in. Whatever Austin thought about, I had no idea.

Finally, we left for the airport.

When it came time to go through security, Austin kissed me long and hard. My mind swooped. His kisses were different from Ronnie's determined, insistent ones. Austin's felt soft and comforting, with a hint of sadness. A bleakness radiated from him, but he forced a smile. "We'll talk soon." He squeezed my forearms as I looked at him.

I stepped away. "Make millions."

If that was what he wanted, I might as well encourage him. His face brightened as he agreed.

* * *

AUSTIN'S SADNESS and Ronnie's intense focus followed me back to Island Park. They were two very different and yet similar guys. Austin's eye was on the money. He was climbing the corporate ladder, and he wasn't going to stop, no matter what he said to me. He wanted me by his side, but he was also an extreme momma's boy, and a relationship with him would always include a woman who didn't like my existence.

Ronnie was free of his parents. He said he loved them, but only saw them once every couple of years because of the physical distance between them. They lived somewhere in the East. Ronnie's eye was on driving and living a life of passion. He was an independent type. I wasn't sure what he wanted with me, or maybe I should say us. "Us" was still new and forming.

On the airplane, I played with my camera, examining the pictures of the racing world. The smells of the burnt tires, the rattle of the cars, the thrill of speed, and the rush of being near Ronnie.

At home, both guys called and texted. I had to struggle to stay focused on cleaning the cabins because of all the distractions those two caused me. Keeping up two relationships was becoming stressful. Austin wanted to know why my phone was busy, and Ronnie called early and often.

* * *

ONE WEEK after my trip to Tucson, JT's office called. I answered in the middle of cleaning a tub. I was actually sitting in the tub scrubbing the titles. "Hello?"

"Looking for Darlene Britain."

I sat up. "Speaking," I said through a tight throat.

"This is Marsha from Cell Towers Incorporated. You applied here a few weeks ago."

"Yes."

"Mr. Devonshire would like to offer you the job if you're still interested." She blurted out my starting pay, which was five dollars more an hour than I was earning cleaning tubs. "Plus, there's a robust health benefit. We require you to go through a company training before you begin. We'd like to know if you're still interested in the job."

I plopped down onto my backside in the middle of the tub. "I— I'm not sure," I said.

"You have twenty-four hours to respond to the offer. I'll be emailing you the details."

I hung up the phone feeling completely confused and pressured to make a decision.

* * *

THE NEXT MORNING, while still in my bed resting and thinking about whether to take the job, a knock sounded on the door. I grabbed my bathrobe, tossed it on, and opened the door to my stepfather.

He wore jeans and a T-shirt and looked ready for the day. "Darlene, it's a perfect time for a four-wheeling adventure. I'd love to go with you as the sun rises."

Jackson had never asked me to do anything alone with him. Currently, my social life had boiled down to the phone, and I was itching to be in nature, even if it was with my stepdad.

Twenty minutes later, we zoomed our four-wheelers down the dirt road that circled the cabins along the Snake River. We left trailing dust clouds following us. Jackson sure could drive fast. It reminded me in a small way of how Ronnie had driven his four-wheeler.

The sun peeked up above the gray mist, casting a red-blue richness over the horizon. The morning was cold, and I had put on my coat, hat, gloves, and black well-worn moon boots.

Surprisingly, no snow covered the ground, but crystal frost sparkled everywhere. I'd need to come back and capture pictures of this. We rode intensely for about an hour before Jackson pulled over to a public picnic area and stopped. He climbed off his four-wheeler, grabbed his backpack, and headed to the picnic table. I joined him, wondering what was going on.

"Your mom made us breakfast." He unzipped his backpack and pulled out toast wrapped in tinfoil, boiled eggs, cut up celery and carrots, and a small container filled with watermelon, strawberries, pineapple, and blueberries.

We began to eat, and I was about halfway done with my

burnt toast when Jackson said, "I have a proposal for you to consider."

My stomach tightened. Since Mom had prepared breakfast, she must have known about it, too. My eyes focused on his serious face, waiting for what he was about to say. This was becoming a thing—people taking me to nature to pop bad news. First, Austin and now Jackson.

I blinked, trying to think what it could be. "You and Mom aren't planning on moving, are you?"

"No." Jackson fiddled with the used tinfoil. "It's nothing like that. I've noticed your love of the camera. You had one when I first met your mom and watching you with the new camera. I see you still have that interest."

I stopped eating and rested my hands on the picnic table as I looked at my stepdad. He had taken off his helmet for breakfast and sported quite a head of hat hair. He spoke deep and with command. I rarely saw this serious side of him. I waited to see where he was going.

"Anyway, I have connections with a photographer. As you know, that was how I earned my living when I met your mother. I made some phone calls. Bottom line, there's a school in LA that's considered to be number one in photography."

My heart leaped... then fell.

I was about to move to Tucson now. He wanted me to do his thing.

Jackson wiped at his red nose from the chill with a napkin. "I think this school would be perfect for you."

My eyes narrowed. How would anyone know what was perfect for me? I didn't even know that.

"It isn't a traditional college, like where your mother

taught. The school is known for being progressive. They encourage debate and experimentation."

Did Jackson think I was progressive? I don't know how he could. After all, I did live with him and Mom, and all I did was clean cabins. Nothing progressive in that. I zipped up the last of my toast in a sandwich bag.

"You would do well there," Jackson continued.

"Why?" I asked.

His eyes flickered. Maybe he wasn't expecting that question. "Because you are always experimenting and thinking."

I let that settle inside me. He might have a point.

"The school was founded by Walt Disney in the sixties, and they're known for designing their education around collaboration and diversity. This is the kind of school I wish I had gone to when I was your age."

Walt Disney created a school? That was cool. Mom had to be the one to put him up to this. She was getting desperate, so she roped Jackson in. She must be worried I'd opt for one of these guys I was dating instead of moving on with my degree. Or, even worse, I'd settle for being a maid forever.

Jackson wasn't done telling me about the school, though. "You'd be free to develop your work. Keep the copyright. They're very involved in growing the students' professional careers. If you earned a degree from there, you'd have many possibilities for your future. The school is based in Santa Clarita, and you'd experiment with a wide range of media. I wish I could do it myself. In the end, you'd walk away with a bachelor of fine arts in photography and media."

"What?" I asked.

"What what?" Jackson asked.

"What are you talking about?"

"I'm talking about you going to school and getting a photography degree."

I stopped cleaning up. "What?"

"That's what you love to do, isn't it? Take pictures."

"Of course. It's a hobby."

"A hobby you could turn into a career if you go to a school like I'm talking about."

That school sounded like a foreign world that would be easy to get lost in. "I'm not sure what I'd do with something like that," I said.

"You don't need the answers. Get the education and then see where it takes you," Jackson said. "You like taking pictures, so what's the problem? It's doing something you love, so if it doesn't work out, at least you were having fun getting the degree."

I picked up the rest of the breakfast. I didn't know what to say. Jackson was going out of his way to tell me about it. I handed him the leftovers. "It sounds really cool. I doubt I could afford it or get in."

Jackson smiled. "I got you accepted and a partial scholarship if you want it. All you need to do is fill out the paperwork."

CHAPTER 10

*P*hotography school. The idea was foreign and not something I'd even considered. I struggled to breathe.

"Give it some thought," he said, leaving it at that.

He had really gone out of his way for me. That meant something. No matter what I decided, it was nice, he had done that.

"Thank you." I meant it and hoped he could feel my sincerity.

He nodded and didn't say anything more until it was time to go back.

Mom greeted us at the back door. Her eyes were wide and anxious. "Well?" she asked as I walked in.

I sat on the wooden bench to take off my shoes. The pressure coming from her was nothing compared to what I'd felt at the racetrack. "The ride was beautiful, Mom, you should've come. We saw several types of birds—"

"What about the school offer?" Mom asked, not wanting to get sidetracked.

I'd face her head-on. "Mom, that was tricky to set Jackson up this time instead of doing it yourself. Scholarship for photography school—that's certainly going all out."

"I had nothing to do with it except to help with breakfast." She brushed some of her hair back. "I had to agree not to pressure you, and that's what I've done."

Mom wasn't behind it? That was going to take me a second to wrap my mind around.

"This was all Jackson's idea."

I looked at my step-dad, who was in the mudroom hanging up clothes and cleaning equipment from the ride. He was probably trying to make himself busy to avoid this conversation.

I lowered my voice. "That was sweet of him."

"So, what do you think?" Mom asked gently like she was coaxing a spooked horse.

I set my jaw tight. I wasn't going to be smothered into a decision. Ronnie said to follow my passion. I'd have to figure out if this was it.

"I don't know," I said.

"Is it something you might want to do?"

There was that question again. What did I want? I thought about the photographers at the racetrack and what it felt like to have the moment take me over, sweep me off my feet. Would this school get me closer to doing more than that?

"It's a big decision," I said.

Mom put her arm around me and pulled me close to her. "It is." She kissed my forehead.

I fought the instinct to push her away. She was being

way too smothering, and that was making it hard to make a decision for my life.

LA versus Tucson.

School versus a job I was offered.

Austin versus being completely on my own.

And Austin versus Ronnie.

All life-changing decisions.

I learned at the track, I could move forward, not seeing where I was headed even with fumes burning my eyes. Time had come for me to grow up and decide my fate, whether I could see the end of the track or not. Time to trust I could figure out the guardrails, and the centerline, and just go on my own.

Mom stood to leave me with my thoughts. "Austin's been calling. He says he needs to talk to you right away."

Yeah, the job.

I called back.

"You got it!" He sounded excited.

I didn't tell him I hadn't decided yet if I'd take it. I didn't tell him about the photography school Jackson just offered.

If I was to shoot photos of how I felt, I'd have a whole collage of blurred images. Austin was still on the phone, wanting to know if he should book the flight out to Tucson. My head swirled. Tucson? School? Choices? All at once, my quiet, boring life had lots going on.

I sat on the stair in the hallway and brushed my foot along the stair in front of me. My life felt very adult-like. I yawned. I needed to go for a run and clear my head.

"I'll be seeing you soon." Austin was acting like every-thing was normal between us, but it wasn't.

I paced up down the stairs, through the living room by

the dying fire, back up the stairs, then to the window to look out onto the trees in our front lawn.

After I hung up the phone, Mom found me sitting on the stairs with tears on my face.

She sat below me, looking up over my knees. "What's going on?"

"Choices."

Mom sighed. "You do have a lot bubbling. Just know you can stay here for as long as you want. You don't have to choose any of them if you don't want to."

I looked up at her and thought about not making a choice. That was tempting to just not choose anything. It wasn't as bad as I thought hanging here with Jackson and Mom, cleaning cabins. It was quiet and peaceful.

I sniffed. That was the old me. I wasn't stuck anymore. I had an idea—a guardrail—where I was headed. "I don't want to stay here."

She nodded like she expected that.

It was time for me to leave the nest.

"One decision down." Mom put her hand on my shoulder.

Yes, one choice down. The job, school, Austin, and Ronnie crowded around me, wanting to be picked. I wiped my eyes to get a clear picture of it all.

"Jackson and I will support you no matter what you do, so you don't have to worry about that. I want you happy and following the right path for you."

That was added pressure I didn't need, but if race car drivers could handle not seeing where they were going at two hundred miles an hour, I could handle not seeing where I was going.

* * *

I CALLED RONNIE. We needed to talk. I needed more information. He was at the racetrack in between runs.

I told him about the job.

"Congrats," he said.

I waited to hear what he really thought about me doing that, but he didn't say any more. His response was completely the opposite of Austin's, who wanted me to pack up for Tucson today. It was also different from Mom's, who comforted me and told me I didn't have to decide. Even Jackson's differed since he had highlighted another path.

"What should I do?" I asked Ronnie.

A car roared in the background.

"I can't answer that," he said after the car noise died down. "That's something you have to answer for yourself."

My chest pounded. How was I supposed to know? Ronnie made everything sound so easy and clear, but it wasn't like that for me.

"But I don't know which path to take."

He sighed. "Sometimes you have to try things out to see if it's a go. I don't know any other way."

That made more sense than I wanted it to. Maybe I needed to go back to Tucson and check it out one more time.

* * *

A FEW HOURS LATER, Ronnie texted me. *Dari, in my mind, I'm thinking of you as my girlfriend. Is that all right with you?*

Girlfriend? The fact Ronnie, the sweet, kind, race car driver wanted me for a girlfriend sent warmth and tingles through me.

I couldn't say no. I texted: *Yes.*

As soon as those words slipped through my fingers, my stomach tightened. Austin. I couldn't string both of them along. I didn't know yet. I hadn't decided.

I couldn't make this decision right now over a text. I had to figure out my work situation. But I wasn't ready to lose Ronnie either. I scrubbed the cabin with extra *oomph*.

Finally, after a lot of window cleaning, I texted Ronnie again: *I can't be exclusive right now, but I can have someone very special in my life. I hope you understand.*

I held my breath and returned to cleaning a cabin, trying not to think. I shook as I cleaned… far more anxious about Ronnie's response than I wanted to be.

Ten minutes later, he texted back: *I do understand. Sometimes, things are very easy for me to decide. You are that decision. If I crowd you too much, I know you'll tell me.*

Heat sprouted through me. He was giving me space. He was trusting me. He was being very mature yet letting me know he was interested. So, I responded back with the truth: *Thank you for understanding. You aren't going to make it easy on me, I can tell.*

He and Austin weren't making it easy on me. Not one bit.

* * *

ON A PLANE AGAIN, but this time no sexy cowboy boarded. Yes, I had to look. Ronnie was in Southern Cali doing some race. He had texted or called me every day and wished me safe travels. I wished him safe driving—really, really, safe driving.

I had barely caught a glimpse of Austin as I descended the escalator when he rushed up and swept me into his arms to dunk me down for a breathless kiss. I couldn't help but laugh. That was quite the greeting in the small Tucson airport.

I was here to interview JT for further information. I wrote to him and requested an extension, so I could fly out one more time to understand the position better.

Austin squeezed me to him tighter. "I missed you," he whispered. "Let's get you to JT's and get your interview over with, so I can have you all to myself."

I ran my hand through his wavy hair as passengers weaved around us. "Are you going to tell me we have to do something with your mom? I'm sure she has come up with some creative ideas to split us apart for this trip."

Austin took my hand and we walked toward the airport exit doors. I had managed to pack extremely light and shove everything in my carry-on bag. "She tried," he said.

I bit down on my lip. I might have to stand up to her this time.

"Relax," Austin said with a laugh. He let go of my hand and massaged my shoulders, which had crept up to my ears. "I stopped her dead in her tracks. There'll be no inter-ference from Mom this weekend. No parties to go to. No commitments. It'll just be me and you, baby, all weekend long, to do whatever we want after the interview."

My hands started shaking. I had wanted Austin to do something like that for a very long time, but it didn't calm my nerves. I peered up at him. "Did you really do that? Really?"

Austin looked at me, slid his arm around my shoulder, and pulled me close to him. "Of course. You're worth it. I want to spend the time you have here with you. In fact, I want to spend a lifetime with you."

My eyes teared up.

He hurried in front of me and grabbed my hands to stop me from walking. He sunk onto the hard, white, shiny airport floor on bended knee. Travelers gave us a doubletake.

I tugged on his arm. "Austin, get up. People are going to think you're proposing. You're making a scene."

We receive many more weird looks. I tugged on his hands. He could be such a prankster at times. "Austin!" I said with insistence.

Finally, I glanced down to give him the eye that hopefully would stop his joking, but I didn't see amusement. I saw a tenderness that stopped me.

"Darlene, will you marry me?" Austin asked. He reached into his shirt pocket but stopped when he saw my face.

My throat constricted. I didn't know what to say. Marriage? Another really big adult thing. My legs went weak. I started to shake.

"Austin…" My voice trembled. "I don't know. I- I—" Tears slipped down my face. "I love you, but…"

He stood and pulled me to his chest. I burst into tears. He stroked my hair. "Shh, shh. I love you, too. We'll figure it out. You don't have to worry about it today."

* * *

In the interview, I was told the position they were considering me for was that of an event planner. I was to manage the reputation of the company by putting on sponsored events where we would educate the public about how to live cleaner and be environmentally conscious.

I'd be speaking, coordinating the speakers, and running the store at the back of the events. I'd also make sure to take all the orders when the company did the upsell. Overall, a very cool opportunity and very different than the job I thought I was applying for.

I was totally going to have to think about it. It wasn't a bad opportunity, but it did come with moving. So, did the school opportunity my stepdad had gotten me. No matter what I chose, it meant a big change in my life. I almost felt up to it.

Austin smiled as I described the job while we strolled to his car. But his smile looked forced since I'd turned down his marriage proposal. He was less talkative and walked slower, too.

I had hurt him by saying no. Well, I didn't actually say no, but I certainly didn't say yes. The truth was, I couldn't say yes.

Marriage? Now, when I was still trying to figure things out? It seemed actually like a desperate move. It might be one of those distractions Ronnie talked about not paying attention to, especially when a person wanted to go after their passion.

While we headed out for dinner, my phone rang. I glanced at who was calling: Ronnie. My chest pounded. Austin didn't need to know about that today. We had agreed it was okay to date others, but I really wasn't sure if it was okay and how he'd feel about it since he just proposed.

Ronnie's call went to voicemail. I felt a twinge of guilt, not talking to him. I did want to know how the race went. By the time I would be available to talk, though, he'd probably be in bed sleeping.

When both doors were shut in Austin's car, I put on my seatbelt to distract myself. I didn't know what to do with the twisting nervousness that consumed me.

Austin started the car and flipped off the radio. He turned in his seat to face me. "Darlene, who's the other guy?"

I looked down at my feet, my vision blurring. "What?"

"I've seen your posts on Facebook, and I know he just called. Who is he?"

My hands fell in my lap. What had I posted on Facebook? Heat rose on the back of my neck. I was going to have to tell him, and it would hurt him. I didn't want to do that, but he deserved to know the truth. Not telling him would hurt even more.

"I know we agreed we could date other people," Austin continued. "I really didn't think you'd do it. I thought you were saying that just to get at me 'cause you were mad I was leaving."

"You weren't wrong about that."

"I didn't think you'd find anyone living in Island Park."

I had thought that, too. The area seriously lacked in the youth department.

"But somehow you managed. You are pretty, so I guess I should have expected it." He rubbed his forehead. "Now, I want the truth." Austin spoke in a soft tone like he was afraid he'd scare me away.

I looked again at my twisting fingers. So, he had known about Ronnie. That explained him standing up to his mom, the marriage proposal, and maybe even this job interview. Austin was worried he was going to lose me. I didn't want a man who only acted out of fear. If I didn't want that in a guy, I needed to be brave in our conversation and face it head-on.

"What do you want to know?" I wasn't going to hide this from him. I wasn't cheating on him. I didn't need to feel this ton of guilt.

"Who is he?"

I was going to answer his questions, but I was also going to stick to the point. I didn't need to give him any unnecessary details, like how my heart fluttered every time Ronnie called. Or how, when we were together, we became a makeout machine, and his intense kisses made my head spin. Or the fact that I felt so alive when I was with him.

"A race car driver," I said.

Austin flinched. "Where did you meet him?"

He sounded amazingly matter-of-fact about this. I thought he would've been much more reactive.

"On a plane."

"To come here?" Austin asked.

I nodded. I could see him putting the details together. I had met another guy while on my way to be with him, a trip he had arranged and gotten his company to pay for.

"Is he why you left the party that one night?"

My chest felt like someone punched it in the center. "Well, not exactly."

"So, yes."

"No. I wanted to experience a racing event. I have never been to one."

Austin ran his fingers through his hair. Maybe to distract myself, I noticed it had grown longer than normal, but was still short enough, so all the hairs fell back into place.

"Let me get this straight." He looked over at me. "I'm not sure what happened."

My heart rate picked up. He was going to want details. I had been so lucky he hadn't asked about it much before. I had just told him I was tired of the party and I didn't mean to worry him. He probably would have asked more, but he had to get to work. We never revisited the topic after that.

He tapped the steering wheel as though to emphasize his frustration. "You took off from a party to go hang with a guy you had just met *on a plane* to go to a race car event on the outskirts of town?"

That sounded awful the way he put it. I avoided his eyes. My neck started to hurt from the strain of hanging my head low. "Um…"

I was getting tired of being put on the spot. He had a part in all this, too. He was the one who insisted on going to a party instead of spending time together. He was the one who had ditched me.

"Do you love him?"

I slapped my hands down on my lap. "Austin," I wailed. "That isn't a fair question."

His eyes searched mine. His lips turned downward as his gaze shot out a glare with an angry intensity. They held a coldness I had never seen. Not once had he gotten like this, no matter what his mom or dad was doing. Not once had I seen him this upset.

"Well, do you love him?" he asked.

I couldn't keep eye contact. I squirmed from the glare. I shifted in my seat then looked back down at my lap. "I don't know."

CHAPTER 11

*D*espite the tension between us, Austin drove safely to a small American café off the main road. He didn't say anything the entire drive. He kept his eyes fixed on the road, and not once did he glance over at me.

My thoughts tossed back and forth. I wanted to look at my phone. I thought I saw on my screen a notification of a voicemail from Ronnie, which he rarely did. Something must be up.

Austin clenched his jaw so tight it looked like he might strain his jaw muscles. He'd get a headache if he wasn't careful. I needed to calm Austin down if we were going to remain friends and somewhat together.

My stomach clenched. I didn't want to lose Austin. It had been me and him forever. He was the one who helped me when my parents divorced, and he helped me when my mom got married to his dad. He had done a good job being there for me… well, until lately.

I took a deep breath to settle the panic fluttering in my

chest. This was confusing. I was hurting people and making a mess by dating two guys. I needed to make a decision now. No more putting it off.

I needed to decide who I wanted to be with. I needed to decide if I was going to take this job that JT just offered me, which seemed like a good opportunity, but so far from anything, I had ever thought about doing. I needed to decide if I was going to go to school. I didn't have much longer until the application was due. I needed to make decisions.

Austin turned the car into a half-filled parking lot of the restaurant. He yanked his keys out of the ignition and shifted into park.

I jerked, startled.

He fiddled with the doorknob and climbed out of the car as I messed with the seatbelt. My panic made it hard to push the release button.

Austin didn't stop to look back or wait for me. He kept going marching into the joint with a firm determined pace.

I grabbed my purse and fumbled it, getting out and closing the door. I took a couple of steps but realized I hadn't locked the door. So, I stepped back again to hit the button that kept our stuff safe.

Puffy bright clouds rolled in the sky, not matching our moods at all and giving me no clue what to do as I tried to keep down the bubbles of panic that swelled in my chest.

The glass door to the café was heavy with smears from lots of small fingerprints on the bottom corner of the door. Once inside, I saw Austin seated on a foam couch, waiting for our table to be called. He didn't look up. I scooted down by him, making sure I didn't get too close, but so it still looked like we were together.

Soon we were called back. I walked by Austin's side, but he still didn't say anything or give any sign he knew I was there. We both ordered waters. After waiting for the waitress, a cute blonde that Austin didn't pay any attention to, we ordered our dinners.

I resisted the urge to glance at my phone and, instead, sat there thinking.

Eventually, I built up my courage. "Talk to me."

Austin gave me less than a thirty-second glance. He leaned against the table and folded his hands together. "There's nothing to say."

The slap of those words made me fall back in my seat. "Yes, there is. I don't want you to be so mad."

Dinner came. We both fell silent. The waitress asked if we wanted anything. Austin asked for ketchup.

When the waitress left to go get it, he jabbed his fork into the meatloaf and jammed it into his mouth, taking big large bites at a time.

I fiddled with my salad. My throat constricted so tightly, it became a battle to swallow the smallest bit. "I not trying to hurt you."

His eyes snapped on me, and I forced myself to meet them.

"Everything has been a mess since you got that new job." I held up my hand. "I'm not blaming you. It's just been a mess, and I know the fact I can't figure out what to do is partly to blame. It just happened all so fast."

"It did," he said.

I flashed him a smile. "Tell me about work today."

He studied me holding another piece of meatloaf on his fork. Something shifted in his face. Maybe the realization that we had a lot of history, and he owed it to me to try to work everything out. He sighed.

"It's a real cool place to work, Dar."

We spent the rest of the dinner talking about his work.

Once we finished eating, he said, "This is our last night together for a while. Do you still want to hang out?"

I smiled up at him. "Sure." I acted like I hadn't turned him down for a marriage proposal or just told him I was dating another guy and wasn't sure if I loved him.

He shook his head. "Why? Why would you want to hang out?"

I grabbed his forearm. He flinched. I pulled my hand away. "Austin, I still care."

"You won't marry me."

"Not yet."

"So, it's still possible?"

My head spun. Now he was pushing for decisions with our relationship. Why hadn't he been like this when he decided to go after his new job opportunity. It would've been easier then. I was clearer on what I thought we were and what I thought I wanted.

"Austin, you're my best friend."

After I said those words, it didn't feel completely true. Lately, I had turned more to Ronnie for support and help. He seemed to be moving into that role of the person I really talked to.

"Who's that other guy?"

I shrugged. "I don't know. A friend."

"A kissing friend?"

My eyes narrowed. "Austin."

He shrugged.

"We agreed to date other people. You were the one who refused to tell me what we had."

Color drained out of his face. "I made a big mistake."

I closed my eyes. That he did. I looked up at him.

"I didn't date anyone else, Dar. I didn't want to."

I crossed my arms over my chest. His words felt accusatory like I had done something wrong. "You talked about us expanding our horizons. You said we needed to see more of the world. You were right, and that's what I'm doing."

"I didn't mean dating other people!"

The volume of his comment caught the entire café's attention. I grabbed his shirt and tugged him toward the door. "Let's talk about it—outside."

We stumbled into the early dark toward the car. My heart knocked in my throat. "Look," I said. "We only have tonight together before I have to go back home. Is this how you want to spend the time?"

"No."

I looked at his sad face. "Austin, I'm sorry. I don't know what I want right now. You're starting to get it all figured out in your life. I hope that I'll get that way, too."

He shoved his hands in his pockets. "How can I help you?"

That was a good question. Not something I had a real answer to. "Be patient with me."

He grabbed my hand and squeezed it. "Okay, that's fair. How about we go to the U of A campus and check it out? It has a photography program."

I stared at him. He was adding to the possibilities of another path I could take. Austin was fighting for me to be with him. That was fair. Throwing photography school into the mix did make it more tempting. I could have Austin, the job, and pursue my art.

"It does?"

He quirked an eyebrow. "I do listen. Jackson is right. A photography program would be good for you. Just do the one here instead of California."

That certainly was an idea.

Austin put his arm around me. "Friends?"

I smiled at him. "Friends."

As we headed to the university, Austin suggested I look up the photography program on my phone.

I pulled it out and saw that Ronnie did, in fact, leave a voice message. I hoped he'd be patient and understanding of me not immediately getting back to him. He'd never put pressure on me about that before, so I felt confident we'd be fine.

I googled photography at the University of Arizona. A few minutes later, I gasped. "They do have a program on photography."

"See," Austin said.

"The program studies nature and the role of photography with it. That's cool." I kept skimming. "They want you to study culture and the history." I skimmed more. "They even offer internships with working professionals. That would be neat."

Austin kept his eyes on the road. "Why don't you do it?"

I sighed. "It's definitely a possibility. I don't know if I could get in. I don't know if I could afford it. There's a lot of things I still don't know." I left out that I didn't know about the other school Jackson had recommended. From the way he talked about, it actually seemed a little less academic and more artsy, which might fit me better.

* * *

WHEN WE DROVE up to the University of Arizona, it was like Austin and I embarked on another exploration together. He hadn't seen the university yet, either. Massive brown and orange brick buildings spread out for miles.

"It's huge." I edged closer to my widow, trying to take it all in.

Austin leaned down to get a better glimpse out the window. "Impressive."

Patches of grass grew between the buildings along with sizable stately palm trees and flowering plants every now and then. "It's so big," I muttered, feeling my stomach knot.

Students stood at a crosswalk with books in their hands even though it was evening. I peered at them to see if they'd give me a clue what it'd be like to be a student there and if I'd like it.

Their faces remained blank and expressionless, and maybe a bit stressed if I was going to guess at an emotion. This place was serious.

"What do you think?" Austin asked.

I swallowed the lump in my throat. "Um…" I peered out the window at the building after building. Others lurked in the background. "This place is overwhelming."

Austin sighed. "You'd get used to it in no time."

Would I?

I shrugged.

"Do you want to walk around to get a feeling of it or dash off to the independent film house and catch an indie movie?"

I had never been to an indie movie house living in Idaho. I wasn't even sure if they had them. "School can wait. The movie house."

Austin gave a forced chuckle. He and I both knew school really couldn't wait.

As we drove to the theatre, I googled California Institute of the Arts, the school Jackson introduced me to.

I read about it again. A private school. Disney founded it. Disney. That was like the complete top of the game. The school was smaller but, from pictures of the campus, the buildings were more unique and fun. Their royal-blue colors and roofs swerved here and there, making unusual designs. On its website, the school claimed to be a game-changer and showed a picture of a girl with blue hair front and center.

Traditional old school versus private and what appeared to be more fun. I sat back in my car seat. This choice, if I could have it my way, was easy. I knew which school was the one for me. The only problem was it was going to disrupt everything with Austin. Dear sweet Austin.

* * *

AFTER THE MOVIE, he took my hand. Our fingers barely touched each others'. The strain between us was still thick.

"Like the show?" he asked.

"Yeah." It was a complete lie.

The movie had been a documentary on an old-time famous rock singer. That was about all I knew about it. I hadn't paid attention to the film. Actually, I couldn't. Too much rattled around in my brain. I had been offered a job, been proposed to, ticked off one of my boyfriends, and now was pretty close to deciding on my future education.

How was I supposed to focus on anything but the whirlwind in my mind?

"I liked it, too," Austin said. "This place is neat. People at work have been talking about it, so I wanted to go and check it out. Thanks for going with me."

"Sure," I said. "It felt like old times."

"It did!" He smiled and stopped me from walking to let a car go by that was maneuvering out of the lot.

"My buddies tell me, once a month the theater holds a film producers' contest where local people make films, and the community gathers to watch them and vote on the best film. We should totally go once you move here."

Austin wasn't relenting. "If I do move out here, that sounds like fun."

This comment pushed Austin back into silence. He pressed his lips together with a hint of a frown. He stayed that way until two cars had passed us. "What time do you have to get to the airport tomorrow? Do you have time for an early breakfast?"

"I have to leave for the airplane at five a.m. Breakfast wouldn't work, but we could go for an early-early morning hike."

Austin looked over at me. "I need to be functional at work."

That made sense, I guess. "What are the hikes like around here?"

He shrugged. "Don't know."

"What? You haven't gone for even a short hike?"

He shook his head. "Working too much."

I tightened my fingers around his. This wasn't the Austin I knew. This wasn't the guy who snuck over to my cabin so early in the morning so many times just so we could see the sunrise.

Now, he wasn't even going outside.

CHAPTER 12

*R*onnie called to invite me out to Salt Lake for a
race if I was willing to make the four-hour
drive. He said he'd pay for the gas and put me up in a sepa-
rate room.

Which was nuts. Drive all the way to Salt Lake to see a
guy I'd met once—well, twice. A guy I'd kissed. A guy who
told me I should follow my passion. A guy who trusted me
to make the drive. He figured I could handle it.

His trust in me was probably the best thing about him.

That and his kisses.

And his blue eyes.

And the way he followed his passion.

There were a lot of good things about Ronnie.

For living in the middle of nowhere, my social life had
suddenly become very active. I was home one week
between flying to Tucson to see Austin and driving to Utah
to see Ronnie. That gave me barely enough time to arrive
home, tell my mom about the job, and discuss the marriage
proposal Austin said was still on the table. I also needed to

talk to her about not doing the job or the marriage and, instead, going to school. We didn't talk about Ronnie because, quite simply, I didn't know how he fit in my life. All I knew was my day wasn't complete unless I talked to him on the phone.

Mom smiled wearily at me. "It seems like you have a lot of directions you could go."

That was it. She didn't argue for one way or the other. The one time I wanted my mom's opinion, she refused to touch it.

Austin now called faithfully every day. He told me he loved me in every single phone call.

I believed him.

Austin suggested that, if I married him, I could take the job and go to school at the University of Arizona. He had checked it out some more. The school had a great reputation.

"Think about it. I want you to be happy. I want you to follow your dreams. This way you could have everything."

Ronnie's reaction to the school and the job was: "Follow your dreams. You only get one life. You won't have regrets if you follow your passion."

"But if I took the job, I'd have a lot of money, and it'd set me up nicely for the future."

"Dari," Ronnie said, his voice strong and commanding over the phone, "money is just money. It doesn't make you happy. You're free to do what you want, but I'd encourage you to do what most makes you happy. My motto is 'to live your life with no regrets.'"

Confusion became my primary emotion over the next few days. I looked forward to vacuuming and wiping sinks.

Cleaning the cabins wasn't asking anything from me. I didn't feel torn when I cleaned. I just went in and did a job I didn't have to think about, and everything looked sparkly when I was done. There was something rewarding about that.

I wasn't going to make a decision. I had to, but I just couldn't. Maybe I could go on forever like this. Talking to Austin in the early evening. Ronnie an hour after that. Going on trips back and forth, visiting the two. I didn't have to choose. I didn't have to grow up yet. I could just enjoy things as they were. I knew I couldn't do that. It was a nice daydream, but I had to choose soon, or everything would blow up in my face, and I would lose it all.

MOST OF THE drive to Utah took place on a freeway with hardly any cars and lots of land that spread out for miles. It allowed me time, every hour or so, to pull over to the side of the road to take pictures. At first, I pulled over for nature sites. The closer I got to Utah, though, the more remote towns filled my camera frame. I liked how the sun played with the way the houses looked. I'd stop to see if I could capture the movement.

A buzz built in me when I stopped to take pictures. I was free. Truly free. What I did on this trip was my choice, and I chose to take lots and lots of pictures. I chose to be on the lookout for another picture.

I chose to stream Celtic Woman music—with its fiddle and divine crisp female voices—to fill my car with magic. The music took me away from my decisions. Instead, I decided to focus on nature, pictures, and singing horribly out of tune to music that transported me to an expanded and whole world.

Ronnie greeted me in the hotel parking lot late Thursday afternoon with that smile that made my whole body tingle. His face looked darker tan and red in spots from being on track.

"Hi," I managed, not able to hold eye contact with his gorgeous blue eyes.

Clearly not interested in chit chat, he engulfed me in his arms and hugged me tightly.

The sweet scent of rustic cologne filled my senses and made my head swoon. "Good to see you," he whispered.

I could feel myself going faint from attraction. I wrapped my fingers around his shirt to hold on as my heart pounded. It gave away just how incredibly attracted to him I was.

"Let's get you settled in your room." He slipped my keys out of my hand and hefted my heavy backpack onto his back like it weighed nothing. He also grabbed my suitcase on one side and my hand on the other.

Our hands joined, connecting into a tight, comfortable grip. I squeezed his palm, feeling a rush from its strength and comfort.

His grasp loosened as my hand wandered up to his palm to his fingertips. His fingers slid down mine again, and in our loose grip, he continued caressing my palm. A shiver ran through me. This hand holding made it hard to walk.

His fingers squeezed down tight onto mine, letting me

know he had me and I was safe. He held it tight for the rest of the walk as we chatted about the drive and his day, spent mostly at the track jawboning and prepping for tomorrow's big race. I talked about my day traveling here, which was uneventful except for the photography. I mentioned the noticeable increase in traffic as I approached Salt Lake, with the Insane drivers ready to plow over anyone in their way.

"Why is everyone in such a hurry?" I asked Ronnie.

He laughed. "It's the way of big cities."

Once we reached the small, rundown hotel room, we kissed again. The short, intense connection ended with me resting my head on his chest, listening to the pounding of his heart.

Breaking away from our embrace, he said, "I'll give you some time and be back in a half hour for dinner."

Before I could respond, he was out the door. I stood there, not sure what to do and struggling to get his kisses out of my mind. Something about them made me lose all track of time.

Slowly, I came back to myself and forced myself to freshen up. That complete, I looked around for my water bottle. When I found it, I realized my car keys weren't near my water where I left them.

I hurried to the window to see if I could spot my car. It was gone.

Panic filled my chest. Had Ronnie taken it? He was a stranger. He could be playing me. Had he stolen my car? What was I going to do if he didn't come back or if it wasn't him who took it?

Trying to stop the shaking in my hands, I called his cell.

No answer. I wiped my forehead as if that would clear out all of my confused thinking.

Should I call the police or wait? If I waited and he did steal my car, I was giving him more time to get away. If he didn't steal it, it would make a bigger mess of everything.

A knock sounded on my door.

I startled, recovered quickly, and hurried to the door to find Ronnie smiling with his black cowboy hat on. "Ready to go?"

Breathing hard, I blinked. "Where are my keys?"

He reached into his pocket and handed them to me. "Something is wrong," he said. "What's wrong?"

Since I had been honest with Austin, I might as well be honest with Ronnie. "I thought you stole my car."

I waited for him to become offended. Instead, a huge smile spread across his face, and he laughed, shoulders shaking.

"That's funny." He reached out and stroked my hair. "Naw, I didn't steal it. I just filled it up with gas and checked it out. Your oil is low, and you had one tire that needed air. I fixed both things. You should be good to go."

Even though I could see he was trying to be nice, it didn't set very well with me. For the first time, I wasn't happy with Ronnie.

* * *

PART OF BEING a race car driver meant arriving at the racetrack to set up camp before the birds had started chirping. This gave Ronnie plenty of time to prep his car and jawbone with his buddies.

As he talked about the weather and the race, I thought about him taking my car. He said he wanted to help me, but that wasn't the kind of help I wanted. I wanted the kind where he believed I could figure it out myself, like he had been doing for all the time I'd been with him.

After about half an hour of talking with his friends, he nodded for me to hop onto his four-wheeler behind him. He leaned into me, and I wrapped my arms tight around his waist, completely forgetting any irritation I had over him taking my car.

As we drove, the other racers looked up from their tinkering to smile and wave. Finally, we stopped at a long red and blue car where Ronnie needed to check-in with Wild Cat Kirkus.

We stopped, and they chatted in the same way most of these conversations went. I heard: "What'd it run yesterday?" and "How much percentage are you going to use?" and "You might need to bump it up a few points because of the air." *Blah dee blah* went the conversation. And I had no idea what any of it meant.

About thirty seconds into their chat, I grew bored and flipped out my camera to snap pictures. There were a lot of things to capture my attention. How could I depict this image in an interesting way? How could I capture the business these car people engaged in?

Ronnie and I were in the middle of doing this mid-morning dance with the day's heat on the rise when a thick, gray-haired man with a large gut pulled up in a golf cart. He wore a navy polo shirt, slacks, and a lanyard that declared his status.

"Cactus Ronnie," he said in a deep, clear, powerful

voice. "Mr. Wilson wants to see you up in the tower now. It's important."

Ronnie stiffened, then looked at me with concern in his eyes. "Will you be okay for a bit?"

The sun had slipped behind a cloud, casting a gray shadow on the morning. The men we were hobnobbing with looked away. One guy cleared his throat. Another suddenly became thirsty and took a drink of his still-steaming coffee. Everything suggested this "talk" put people on edge.

Lots of bustle started behind us with the motion of people moving in every direction and engines being cranked to life.

Of course, I didn't want Ronnie to leave me here with all these strange older men, but there was no way I would cling to him or hold him back from doing his business. I could handle myself.

I held out my hand. "Would you mind giving me your keys so I can retreat to your truck if I get too hot?" I asked. The sun had already started to cook me, and it wasn't even ten in the morning. It had to be getting near to eighty degrees already.

Ronnie handed the keys over, gave me a short kiss, and left. I nodded at the gear-head guys who stood with coffees in hand, not saying anything, but all watching me. I had suddenly found myself plopped into the middle of an exclusive guys club, uninvited.

I cleared my throat. They continued to regard me with cold disinterest shuffling their feet and biting their lips. Even though the morning light still encircled us, and it was definitely too early, I muttered, "I'm going to get a taco."

I bolted toward the food booths, glad to put distance between me and the old racers. They were fine enough when I was with Ronnie but, with him gone, it grew awkward fast. I was a girl and also younger than most of their daughters.

It didn't take long to stumble onto the lane of food booths. They were about eighty feet long behind the bleachers, constructed out of metal campers or wooden shacks. Most of the booths looked like this might be one of their last days before completely crumbling into shambles.

Along the lane, signs were strung up advertising upcoming events and insurance promotions. These ads added to the track's interior perimeter created a chaotic casual homestyle feel.

Since it had been hours since Ronnie and I had eaten a little bacon and toast, I was hungry. The options for food were limited to one form of grease or another, with the occasional offering of dried-out cookies, brownies, or sandwiches.

Gettng a taco turned out to be the best option, even though it was only ten in the morning. Wondering how long Ronnie might be, I piled fresh onions and cilantro onto the lifeless meat, offering it a spice lift.

While devouring the small corn taco, I took in this new world of people so fascinated with race cars. I didn't really understand it, but I could appreciate their excitement.

Maybe this was how I would feel if I pursued the photography program in California. I could totally geek out about photography. Jackson and Austin were right about that. My stomach knotted. I had submitted my papers to Disney University. I closed my eyes. Jackson said he had gotten me in. I guess soon I'd find out if that was the truth.

Once I was done with the taco, I looked around at the spectators, feeling very much the foreigner. Ronnie was taking a while. I snapped a few pictures of the porta-potties, wondering if I could use the pictures as some kind of commentary on track life.

I had taken my first round of shots and was about to go into another frenzy when strong arms encircled my waist. I squirmed around to find Ronnie holding me with the biggest smile I had ever seen on him.

"Hi." I flushed.

"Having fun?" he asked.

I looked down at the camera in my hand. "Waiting for you and thinking about my college application."

He took that in and nodded like it made sense. He was bouncing on his tiptoes like something was up.

"What took so long?"

His smile widened. "I just received an offer to go pro."

That took my breath away. Pro. That was a big deal.

"Wow! Congratulations."

He beamed. "They'll pay for my year of touring, expenses, everything. They're buying a two-hundred-mile-per-hour billboard. I've wanted this for a long time."

We stood close to the gate between the food booth and vendors, whose tables mostly overflowed with T-shirts and hats. People passed us, sipping on pop and carrying trays of nachos or fries. Their ordinary lives paled next to Ronnie's big news. He was really moving up in his world.

The sun had risen enough behind Ronnie that I had to

squint to make him out. The joy radiating off him was contagious.

"That's so-o-o cool."

He slapped his hands together. "This is huge. This is the dream."

I blinked in the sun. "So, I take it you'll have lots of time talking with engines."

He nodded. "Sure will. I'll have the best engines. The high performing ones. I have a top-notch crew."

I wrapped my arms around him. "I'm so happy for you," I said as ecstatic as I could be. Despite how thrilled I was for him, I couldn't stop the fear from creeping into my chest. Pro status meant things would change, and we might not be together anymore.

He gave me a kiss and pulled away. "Looks like we both have opportunities to pursue."

Me? I wasn't sure what he was talking about. I guess my opportunities included school or work. Neither of those sat on the same level as going pro as a race car driver.

He gently rubbed my back with his hand. "This is good," he said softly. He squeezed me tight as some old-timers approached to congratulate him.

"Finally, they told you." One of the guys slapped Ronnie on the back.

Ronnie smiled. "They sure did."

The guy took a sip of their beer from a plastic cup. "It was hard not telling you. You have the gift, and you deserve this."

On and on went the celebration.

Three hours later, when I saw a child reading a book, I

realized Ronnie must have meant schooling as my opportunity. He must be thinking that was the one I'd choose.

How did he know I would do that? Maybe it was
because he didn't know about the other job interview or
the marriage proposal. If I tried to bring any of it up, he'd
say it wasn't his business.

We left it at that, which resulted in confusion for me as
to what "we" were. On race day, there was no time to
worry about relationships, my future, or any of that
personal stuff. All our focus needed to stay on helping
Ronnie make it down the track as many times and as fast
as possible.

I was starting to like my part in that. The higher the sun
rose, the faster he soared down the lane, even though other
racers said it was hard to do that. He was on a high, and
nothing could stop him.

By early afternoon, Bill let me drive the four-wheeler
down the frontage road by myself to pick up Ronnie at the
end of the track. I'd do that, and while I waited for him to
pack up the parachute, I snapped more pictures.

Ronnie had been able to get me a photographers' wrist-
band. With it, I was allowed to come close to the wall when
he was on the track. I approached the cars and the wall
every time I could, taking as many pictures as possible as
Ronnie strove to make it to the semi-finals.

Late in the afternoon, I parked the four-wheeler off to
the side of the frontage road and hurried toward the
collection of photographers to capture Ronnie and his car
inching up to the starting line in the distance.

In the frame of the picture, I could make out Bill giving
hand signals. *Snap. Snap. Snap.* Ronnie did the tire-spinning

thing, again. *Snap. Snap. Snap.* Tons of smoke hovered over the wheels, covering the car and making it impossible to take a clear picture. I kept snapping, hoping for a magical, eerie image of motion.

The race cars backed up and rumbled as they staged, prepared to take off. I continued to take pictures, ignoring the nerves that ramped up in my chest every time he tore down the track.

The fierce, angry noise the cars emitted rattled my soul, but I held firm, not moving. I wanted pictures of Ronnie roaring down the lane on the day he turned pro. He'd love having them. A memento of sorts of our time together before he launched out into the professional realm. A tear surfaced in the corner of my eye. I was certain it was from all the fumes, not the thought of Ronnie moving on from me.

The cars tore off. Ronnie raced in the left lane again. The powers that be preferred to put him there. The front of his car lifted high as he kept going. I was no longer looking into the camera as I snapped.

"Come on, Cactus Ronnie," I yelled.

The fierce machine jumped and brushed the wall, releasing the roar of metal scraping concrete.

The audience gave a collective gasp.

We all stared at the mangled car.

"Come on, Ronnie," I whispered, tears now free-flowing.

My throat constricted. My eyes fastened on the dented tin.

Was he okay? I didn't know what I'd do if he were hurt —or dead. My hands immediately went to prayer position.

Please be okay. The emergency crew scurried down the track toward the car. Smoke surrounded it.

My vision had blurred as I held my breath. "Come on," I whispered. Then suddenly, from the midst of the wreckage, a black suit emerged. Ronnie lifted his hand and waved.

"He's alive," I gasped.

He limped with two track personnel assisting him off the track. I raced for the four-wheeler, climbed on, and drove like crazy over to where the ambulances were stationed at the start of the track.

I parked off to the side and ran up to the guard, who held out his hand to stop me.

I gasped, "I need to see Ronnie."

The middle-aged man with a bulging stomach held out his hand. "Stop right there."

I glimpsed the top of Bill's head behind him. "Bill," I called out. The desperation or maybe panic dripped heavy in my voice.

Bill saw me and hurried over. "She's okay," he said to the track official. "Let her through."

My pulse pounded double-time, and my lungs constricted as I prepared to find out just how bad it was. I turned to Bill. "Where is he?" My voice choked out in a harsh whisper. More tears flooded my cheeks.

Bill looked at me. "You saw him walking. He's fine. They're going to check him over." He pointed toward the back of an ambulance. The back doors were open. Ronnie, still in his black fire suit, lay on a stretcher hunched down among medical supplies and paramedics. Relief poured through me at seeing him, and I hurried over.

I climbed into the ambulance and scooted past the doctor, who was examining something on his knee. When close enough, I threw my arms around him and sobbed into his shoulder. "Are you okay?"

He smiled. "Just a few bruises. Nothing to worry about."

RONNIE'S CAR would be in the shop for a long time. But they had the best nitro engine builder on it, Rick MacDonald. He was famous throughout the world for his ability to make these engines roar, and Ronnie couldn't stop talking about how cool it was to have "The" Rick MacDonald's hands on his engine.

As he spoke and chatted, I nodded. Ronnie, Bill, and a lot of the guys had all gathered at a breakfast joint after the races to rehash war stories.

Ronnie gave me a curious glance. He whispered, "You okay?"

I seized his arm and rested my head on his shoulder. It was enough just to feel his pulse. The guys kept talking until a famous driver strutted into the restaurant, and they all piled out to greet him.

I stayed in my chair, not trusting my legs and also allowing Ronnie space to hang with his friends. I looked up to see Bill, who remained seated at the same booth.

"It's frightening to see the reality of these machines, isn't it?" Bill asked.

Tears filled my eyes. This definitely wasn't the place to cry, but I couldn't help it.

"I was so scared," I said. "I didn't know if we'd lost him."

Bill fingered his beer. "I felt the same way." He choked up. "Don't know what I'd do without Ronnie. He's a good friend." He shook his head. "He loves this stuff. He wouldn't feel really alive if he wasn't doing this."

I had ordered chamomile tea, hoping it would calm my overreactive stomach. I took a sip. Bill was right. Ronnie's passion for racing was one of the things that had drawn me to him. That was so different from Austin's commitment to ensuring a secure future.

What was my commitment to?

The whole reason I visited Tucson was to get out of the house, but that didn't seem to be enough. What would give me a focus like Ronnie's and Austin's? Could it possibly be photography?

Bill set his beer can down. "The woman Ronnie ends up with will have to understand he'll give the shirt off his back, and he'll love her unconditionally, but she will need to let him roam. He will give her the same courtesy." He looked at me head-on. He was trying to tell me something, a reason behind his words. Heat crawled up my neck.

He cleared his throat. "I probably shouldn't say anything, but I'm going to anyway. There's something special between you and him. I can just see it. There's a sweetness in the way you two interact. It's like you two have finally found each other. I have a good feeling about you two."

The guys rejoined us just after he said that, sparing me a response.

I took Ronnie's arm and held on to it. He reached his hand down to my knee and squeezed it until I jumped.

He laughed.

"Don't," I whispered to him, not wanting to draw attention to us.

The guys continued to laugh. Someone asked Ronnie what he thought went wrong.

"Maybe I wasn't straight on the starting line when I staged the car."

"No, I bet a loose oil line sprayed oil onto the tire," one of the guys countered.

I leaned up into his ear and whispered, "Do you want to look at my pictures of the run?"

He flipped back in his seat, knocking me back. "You shot photos of the run?"

My eyes widened. I nodded.

"Can I look at them?"

I pulled out my camera and found the pictures of the race before handing it to him. I had to remind him which button to push to flip through the photos. He wanted to know if he could get a closer look at a certain shot, so I enlarged the photo, zeroing in on the tires and the front end.

His hand banged the table. "One rear tire is larger in diameter than the other. That steered the car right into the wall. Someone grabbed a mismatched set of tires. It was a crew member error. That makes sense."

I HAD GROWN tired from the chatter of the racers, stories, and questions about cars. I just wanted to be with Ronnie by his side, knowing he was alright. I wanted to enjoy this time I had with him. He was alive. That was important. Not something I could take for granted.

My eyes grew extremely heavy. I closed them, leaning against Ronnie's arm. Instead of taking in my time with him, I fell asleep again, despite the fact we sat in the middle of a busy diner.

What seemed like hours later, he gently nudged me awake, his woody cologne brushing by me. It had a nice rustic aroma I could curl up into all night long.

"Can I borrow your jacket?" I asked.

"What?" a quizzical look on his face, "Why?"

"So, I can smell you when I'm away from you."

He took a finger and ran it down my nose. "Sure, sleepyhead."

He took it off and wrapped it around me. I snuggled into it as he whispered, "We need to talk."

I picked up an undercurrent to his tone like Austin had when he wanted to say something serious.

Worried about what it could be about, I sat up straighter in the leather restaurant booth, stretched, and started to wake up.

The other guys were gone. I glanced at my watch to see that it was early in the morning.

"Tell me how you're doing." I yawned.

He smiled. "A little banged up but good. Occupational hazard."

I stared at him. He was joking about crunching into a wall. "Occupational hazard?" A huge lump rose in my throat. I shivered as I thought of the possibility of him not walking away from the car one of these times.

"That's a bit risky, don't you think?"

"My mom does."

I blinked. He'd never said much about his family.

"She doesn't like it?"

Ronnie sat back on the bench. "Not at all. She refuses to come to my events."

That I could understand. I stroked his arm, letting his thick black hairs bend under my fingertips.

"How does this accident affect things?" I asked.

He scooted to the side to get a better glimpse of me. "What do you mean?"

"Are you still going to be a professional racer?"

He took a finger and wiped at a crumb on the tabletop. "Should be. I can't guarantee anything. There's no such thing as a guarantee in the racing world, but it should be a go. Everyone trades paint with the wall now and then."

A wave of tension rushed through me. Of course, he wasn't going to do anything different. This risk was real to him, and he was willing to take it every time he climbed behind the wheel. Just because he had crashed that wouldn't change anything.

I didn't live my life that way. If things seemed risky, I'd turn around and go the other way. Should I take more risks, or was he wrong in the way he did things? Racing and the thrill of that wasn't worth his life.

He leaned his shoulder into mine, bumping me. "I can tell you're thinking. Tell me what's going on."

"You scared me today."

He fingered his coffee mug in front of me. "Scared me, too. I think it also scared Bill."

"But... you could have..." My throat clogged up.

He leaned into me. "I know."

I stroked the table as I found the courage to speak up. It was time to not hide what I was thinking. "You could die."

Tears rose in me like swelling bread dough. My body shook. There went my plans for having fun together for the time we had left.

"Oh," Ronnie whispered, "sweetie, I'm okay."

He tried to pry my fingers from my face but didn't succeed, so he wrapped his arms around me and pulled me into him. I heard the pounding of his heart—strong pronounced beats.

Another whiff of his woody smell surrounded me, calming me like early morning rain. My body shook.

"Oh, sweetheart." He kissed me on top of my head.

He continued to hold me for a long time. The warmth of his embrace engulfed me.

"My mother said racing was bad on her heart."

I pulled from his embrace. "I get it." I wiped at my eyes.

He studied me. "I have chosen to live my life with no regrets. If I walked away from racing, not knowing what was possible for me to achieve, I'd regret it."

"I understand," I said.

"Do you?" he asked.

I nodded.

"Can you be with someone like that?" he asked.

That was a serious question. "I love that about you."

He put on a smile. "And…"

"And I think I have to figure out who I am to answer that completely. See if the real me fits that lifestyle."

Ronnie drew silent as I tried to answer that question about myself. I was getting close.

"But for now, I certainly see it working. I just can't…"

Ronnie reached out and took my hand. "That's good enough for me."

Our eyes connected, and I knew. Finally, I was on the right path.

He leaned in and kissed me. "Shall we go?"

I squared my shoulders like I had seen my mom do over the years before she dove into uncomfortable situations. "We need to have a talk."

His eyes snapped over to the front door then back to me. "Now?" he asked as though looking for a way out, even though he had been the one who'd first brought up the need to talk.

Through the window, the thick gray soup of night wrapped around the restaurant. The waitress worked by the cash register but, besides her, we were the only ones left in the restaurant. She was probably waiting for us to finish so she could wrap up and go home.

The clock inched close to one in the morning. Despite all that, I held firm. It was time for me to decide. I bit my lip. I had been resisting making decisions for a long time, just floating along.

Doing that wasn't fair to Austin. This was far bigger than a job, or school, although both those things were important. I needed to first figure out what I wanted for me, then decide between two men who loved me. Or choose a school. Or a combination. To go on like I had been wasn't fair to Austin, at the very least. Ronnie seemed more okay with it, but of course, he didn't really know about Austin. He had never asked.

To summon up the courage to confront this, I squeezed my finger. To make the best decision, I needed the facts. At least that was what I told myself as I sat in that diner. Because I really didn't know what Ronnie wanted.

Maybe I was deluding myself that he wanted anything more than a causal relationship. Assumptions were bad in situations of the heart. Mom told me, assuming things had gotten her and Dad into trouble. It'd be hard going back home and not really know where Ronnie was with all this.

I rubbed the back of my neck. I could do this. Even though I didn't know how or what to say, I needed to do this. I bit my lip again. This wasn't going to be easy, but I had to do it if I didn't want to beat myself up for being a chicken and not speaking up.

"I'm leaving first thing tomorrow morning to get back to work, and I'd really like to have this conversation in person. I've been putting it off."

Ronnie picked up a straw that still had its wrapper on it and tapped it on its end. "Okay, shoot."

My chest squeezed tight. He wasn't making this easy on me. "I need to know where we stand. I know you consider me your girlfriend, but I want to know what you want with us."

He tapped the other end of the straw. "What do you mean?"

Ugh. Men, all men, could be so frustrating. This was hard enough to even get out. Couldn't he help me? "I need to know where you want our relationship to go. Do you want us to be boyfriend-girlfriend, dating others or not dating others?"

He raised his eyebrows as though he was confused. "I thought we liked each other."

The tightness in my chest increased and rose to my

throat. "I know that, but I need to make serious decisions about my life. I need to understand where we stand and where we are heading so I can make them."

He tapped the straw twice before saying, "Make any decisions you want. Do what's right for you. I'll never hold you back."

"No," I said, squeezing his arm. "I need to know what *you* want."

He smiled. "I want you to be happy."

He was being elusive. "But what about us?"

The straw fell out of his hand and landed onto the dirty table. "Us can be what you want it to be. I'm not going to tell you what to do."

"Then don't take my car without asking."

His brows furrowed. "What?"

I took a second to steady my nerves. "I know you were trying to be nice by filling my car up, but it freaked me out. More importantly, it showed that you didn't trust I could take care of myself."

Ronnie coughed. When he recovered his breath, he said, "I certainly didn't mean to send that kind of message. I was just trying to make life easier for you."

My shoulders eased down a notch. I continued to look at him, my lips pressed together.

"Hey, I'm sorry. I won't do that again."

"Okay," I whispered, glad to get past it. "You didn't answer my question. What do *you* want?"

"I already told you, for you to be happy."

"Yeah, but what do you want for us? If things were the way you wanted, what would it look like? Do you want us together? Do you want us just to be friends? Do you want us to be committed? What?"

His blue eyes bore into mine. "Darlene, I'm not going to tell you what to do. I don't do that."

I rubbed my face hard, hoping to wipe away my frustration. "Do you still want to date me?"

"Of course."

"I told you before I'm also dating another guy."

"Okay," he said, his voice flat.

My hand slapped the white table. "Say something."

He took a sip of leftover water, then looked at me. "I want to date you for as long as you want to date me. I'm not going to date anyone else. You're free to do what you want. I just don't want to hear details."

"Austin asked me to marry him. He wants me to take a job in Tucson and be with him."

Color flushed through Ronnie's face. He stared at the saltshaker for a long time. "Are you going to do that?" he asked without looking at me.

It was my turn for my shoulders to lower and look defeated. "No. He's not the right guy. Couldn't anyways. Not ready for marriage."

Ronnie shrugged. "Neither am I." He fiddled with his fingers. "I love you, and I want to be with you, but I've got to focus on my racing. This life isn't for families."

His words hung in the air heavy.

A tear appeared in the corner of my eye.

"Considering everything, if you want to hang with someone else, Darlene, I'm not going to hold you back."

He looked so sad when he said that. I knew it came

from his heart. I could feel how much he didn't want to step on my toes. He wanted me to be free to choose.

For some reason, this reaction made me love him even more as I looked at him, face pink and jaw tense. I remembered the panic I'd felt when I thought I'd lost him, and I realized this man was the one I wanted, even though he hadn't proposed and wasn't ready for marriage. Well, neither was I.

I wanted him, even though I had been with Austin longer and knew what a good guy he was. Austin had been trying so hard to become what I wanted, but I'd never felt as drawn to him as I was to Ronnie.

Ronnie didn't have to try. He had a strong independence about him. He had such a solid commitment to his art. I couldn't walk away even if it meant there wouldn't be as much money, even if it meant he'd be in danger every time he raced.

I stared at him, admiring his passion, his commitment, his rock-solid nature. That was what I wanted. I shifted in my seat and crossed my legs on the bench. "Let's say," I said, "I wanted to date only you. What would you say?"

"Darlene, I can't make that decision for you."

"No, you can't, but I made it, and I only want to date you if you can handle only dating me. Along with my extreme focus on photography and me being in photography school."

Ronnie looked into my eyes to see what I was really saying. I hoped he could read in my eyes I had chosen him. I chose my dream, and I chose to be happy.

"I would love that." Ronnie's jaw relaxed. "Let's take it one day at a time. Me racing. You doing school and photography, and us staying connected. I've a good feeling about where this could go."

I had that very same feeling. For the first time in a very long time, I felt on the right path.

We kissed for a very long time, preparing for what was to come.

Continue with the *Millionaire Romance* series … https://
amzn.to/2MI4r4q

Thank you for joining me on the *Millionaire Romance* journey. If you enjoyed the novel, I would very much appreciate you posting a review on Amazon.

https://amzn.to/3r5Rws4

Sign Up…

Romantic Rants Newsletter

and receive an ebook *Husband Shopping,* which explores what we can learn from reality tv on how to attract a man.

https://www.authoranastasiaalexander.com/

ABOUT THE AUTHOR

Anastasia Alexander doesn't have the answers to life's love questions. What she does know is that love in the 21ˢᵗ century is complex. There are no easy answers, and there is richness and juiciness in exploring all the complexity that love brings.

Her credentials are two failed marriages and a current successful marriage (fingers crossed), equaling thirty-one years of marriage and a willingness to believe that the benefits of flirting aren't dead. Since she loves her current husband too much to flirt outside of marriage, she pours her love for flirting into stories.